SEASONS OF THE JACARANDAS

Anthology of Stories Set in Kenya

Elizabeth Orchardson-Mazrui

Published by New Generation Publishing in 2014

First Edition

Cover designed by author.

ISBN: 978-1-910162-81-1

www.newgeneration-publishing.com

 **New Generation Publishing**

CHAPTER ONE

Kenia

My name *Kenia* is both sweet and painful, a bittersweet concoction of all that I am.

I am named for the expansive ochre-coloured savannah grasslands, which, in bright tropical sunlight, become seas of shimmering gold; a miraculous wonder of nature; a reflection of my country, of my soul.

I am named for the second highest mountain in Africa with its magnificent snow-capped peaks, sadly now being depleted by global warming. I am named for the dying springs of degraded water-catchment forests, which, according to my grandparents, long ago beautified our landscape and gave our people abundant crops.

I am named for our straggly, semi-urbanized dusty village with its assortment of ramshackled buildings, mud-and-wattle shacks, and carton and plastic dwellings, a testament to our 'modernity', to our 'development'; pitiful evidence of our poverty.

Above all, I am named for bountiful blessings and the aspirations of my family. My mother is unshakeably certain that one day, armed with certificates, diplomas, and degrees, I shall lift them out of poverty; even stipulating that I will buy them a posh car to show off in. No one heeds my sulky grumbles that my name is synonymous with heavy burdens and blame games. Unfailingly, my grandmother points to the far horizon and urges me to look for the many silver linings that constantly illuminate my name. When I faithfully follow her instructions, joy saturates my entire being; I bristle with happiness that my name is **Kenia**.

When I was young, I believed all was well with my world because of a solitary jacaranda tree growing on the road reserve near our compound. Its astonishing mauve-blue blossoms constantly captivated me. The tree was a reflection of me, *Kenia*. It had endured unbelievable hardships to grow into a robust, lovely tree. I called it *my tree*. Despite its chopped-off limbs and woebegone, bedraggled look, I always considered it a thing of enduring beauty. When stripped off its leaves, I imagined it to be a bizarre being from outer space waiting for someone to clothe it with its purple robes. When in full bloom it was a veritable feast for my tired, hungry, disillusioned young eyes.

Each evening, when I returned from school, I examined the jacaranda tree, looking for the slightest evidence of someone having dared to touch it. If I saw that even the tiniest branch had been snapped off, I challenged others, in a terse voice, to dare cut off another branch; I would whack them so hard their heads would reel, spin, and snap off. Regardless of my dire warning, I always found a branch hacked or snapped off, no doubt for firewood or for chasing away errant goats and troublesome children. Each time I saw this, I wept that the entire tree would one day altogether disappear. Taking no chances, I planted several jacaranda seedlings in our tiny plot, fervently praying they would one day become big trees to provide shade in our bare compound as *my tree* had done for years.

My tree was always uncomplainingly multi-functional – it was the climbing frame for boisterous children and the resting place for men and women, its wide canopy of fine fern-like leaves providing a welcome shady spot for all types of gossip, rumours, and clandestine trysts. It was the provider of bits of wood for cooking, for sweeping compounds and for carving sculptures. Above all, it was the hallmark of our semi-

4

urbanized village *Mirema* alias *Officially* alias *Matopeni,* and now rhythmically pronounced as one word - *MiremaOfficiallyMatopeni*. People constantly plopped beneath my jacaranda's welcoming shade without so much as a polite 'may I sit under your tree?'

Whenever the tree's delicate fern-like leaves gave way to a mass of mauve-blue blossoms, it was a sign that any time soon the rains would come and replace the grime and dust of our environs with gooey mud, which, surprisingly, we all welcomed because the man-made dust ruined our lungs and homes. The dry season gave birth to whirlwinds which spun plastic bags, milk packets, and all manner of rubbish here and there, smothering the surroundings and clothing the straggly shrubs until they looked like bizarre brides, grooms, and bridesmaids gaily dressed for their weddings. The rains were our welcome succour. We children whooped, turned cartwheels, and wallowed in the red mud, happily splashing our way through the choked roads and paths.

Over the years, I have watched our village *MiremaOfficiallyMatopeni* become a semi-urban trading centre with its ever-mushrooming cardboard and plastic-covered shanties and kiosks, ramshackled semi-permanent buildings, Indian-style *dukas*, and on the periphery, a few spectacular mansions with well-trimmed fences and luxuriant shrubs and flowers growing along the entire length and breadth of the high parameter walls, both inside and outside. I have always been intrigued that all this *development* appears to silently take place as we sleep. Many times, I have wondered if a magician helps the newcomers, who must surely creep into our midst like proverbial thieves in the night. Where do they come from? What attracts them to settle in our sprawling *MiremaOfficially-Matopeni*? Do they Google the name to find directions? Do they use a GPS to get to our neighbourhood? The train of these niggling questions keeps me awake night after night.

A long time back, I pestered my maternal grand-mother, who has always lived with us, to tell me the history of our village, *MiremaOfficiallyMatopeni*. According to her recollections, a long, long, long time ago, people called the village *Mirema* after the ubiquitous spindly, dark-barked gnarled trees with their all-embracing canopies of red-tinged green leaves. At some point in time, people discovered that Mirema wood was excellent for making long-burning charcoal; so, over the years, bit by bit, people cut down the trees to make this valuable fuel. Before this wanton destruction, Mirema village was a veritable paradise with a multitude of indigenous trees and plenty of springs and streams with crystal-clear drinkable water. So she says!

Now, looking for springs, streams and mature Mirema trees in our urbanized village is like digging for gold in Kakamega. Even when tiny Mirema seedlings sprout, they are unable to withstand the brutality of a million feet trudging to and fro in search of employment in the city. What chance do tiny seedlings have against the hurrying feet of desperate people who scuttle out of their dwellings like a million ants scurrying to forage for food before the sun gets too deadly hot. In the evening, the people return empty-handed and disillusioned, their sweaty feet cracked and raw from walking the tarmacked streets of the city. Yet, well before dawn the next day, they embark on their various cruel journeys, hoping against hope that on this day they will surely find work.

When I was younger and inquisitive, Father, with bleary, blood-shot eyes, delighted in recounting to me the *real* history of *MiremaOfficiallyMatopeni*. I must have heard the story at least a thousand times, but at every opportunity, I leaned closer to Father, eager to hear it all over again. Over his illegally-brewed alcoholic beverage, Father would tell me that once upon a time,

Mirema was a serene village with so many Mirema trees it was hard to make one's way through the dense forest. Father told me rivers ran here and there like mischievous children in search of adventure. Lamenting the loss of these rivers, he would sigh heavily, take a long swig of brew and say that the name of our village changed from *Mirema* to *Officially* to *Matopeni* and not from *Mirema* to *Matope* to *Officially* as some people liked to claim. Enthralled, I listened keenly, eagerly inhaling in the pungent smell of his brew which teased my nostrils in a strange, tingling way. He once gave me some to sample, but it tasted so disgusting, I puked it all up under his favourite Mirema tree. He wasn't at all amused that I had had the audacity to throw up his precious brew, but grudgingly said the puke was good for the tree; laughing hilariously that perhaps the tree would get so drunk, it would sprout new branches and leaves and dance around the village like a possessed demon. I laughed hilariously.

My mother had a much more interesting story about the three names of our village. According to her, when a Colonial Administrator arrived in the village to survey the land and to mark out boundaries, he openly admired the spindly, rough-barked Mirema tree, asked for its name, seemed delighted with the word and imperiously informed the people that from that day forth, the name of the village would be *MIREMA*. Mother said the sweaty red-faced white administrator, with his head protected by a white pith helmet, scribbled something on paper, pointed to it several times and said loudly '*Mirema!*' When the African Colonial Assistant Clerk of Works explained to the curious villagers what the white man was saying, they laughed uproariously, some spitting contemptuously that the *muthungu* actually had the nerve to suggest that they, the elders and custodianians of history and traditions of the entire village, were ignorant fools who did not know the name of their own village.

One elder exclaimed, 'why does he have to tell us that? We have always called our village Mirema from time immemorial!' The Assistant Clerk of Works told the Colonial Administrator what the elder had said. Authoritatively, the white man pointed to his paper and said '*Mirema – Officially*.' Soon after, people began to call Mirema '*Officially*'.

The name *Officially* stuck for decades until a new generation renamed it *Matopeni*, on account of the mountains of sticky red mud during the rainy seasons. At some point, some people changed the name to *MiremaOfficiallyMatopeni*, pronounced as one word in a singsong way. When Mother pronounces the name, she does so like a seasoned rap singer. The youth, to be quite contrary, call it *MatopeniOfficiallyMirema* or *OfficiallyMatopeniMirema* or other combinations.

Our village storytellers recount that long before the colonialists came, Mirema had been a quiet, gentle sort of place where nobody ever seemed in any particular hurry. Not only did Mirema trees grow in profusion, but other indigenous trees of all types covered the entire landscape. Trees and shrubs sprouted practically overnight due to the underground springs. Apart from occasional droughts, the rains were usually reliable and the land was fertile. Harvests were plentiful, giving people enough food and a generous income when sold at market places. People woke up early, drank their fermented millet porridge, ate sweet potatoes or yams, and went about their chores, singing, laughing and exchanging pleasantries with their neighbours.

Each day, the young boys drove the livestock from their shelters and moved leisurely in search of fodder, while the young girls went in search of water and to gossip and discuss their boyfriends. Even the village free-range chickens scurried here and there, frenziedly scratching and unearthing worms, which they gobbled greedily, growing nice and plump. With saliva dribbling from their mouths, the elders said that when roasted, the succulent chickens, served with traditional vegetables and *ugali,* was a rare treat enjoyed by one and all. Men sat under the shade of the gnarled Mirema trees and discussed all manner of things. The storytellers claimed that gossip, rumours, rivalry and neighbourly discord helped to break the monotony of the good life. When neighbours quarrelled, the elders called meetings and resolved the disputes to everyone's satisfaction.

Children chased each other boisterously, darting in and out of snoring elderly men lying supine under Mirema trees, while women and girls rhythmically pounded grain, their faces awash with perspiration. All children belonged to the community and anyone could chastise them, so long as people did so in a loving manner and not out of malice. No one mocked childless women and men because they were parents to countless number of Mirema children. My grandmother, with a click of her tongue, likes to emphasize that nowadays women and men are mocked if they have no children of their own and that some men shamelessly chase away childless women from their matrimonial homes. 'That never happened in my day!' my grandmother says in disgust, sending a jet of spittle into the nearby bushes. In my own mind, I wonder about the accuracy of all these varied stories; often wanting to blurt out questions, but usually hold back out of respect for my elders and their recollections. My mother has drummed into me enough times how rude it is for youngsters to question elders.

Nowadays, late in the evening, as the smell of food pervades the air, the communal fire near the jacaranda tree beckons people to congregate around it for yet another night of stories. Keenly, I listen to elders reminiscing about the 'good old days'. I see their eyes follow the children play hide and seek when they tire of the stories.

Indulgently, they watch them, not once reprimanding them for their raucous laughter and fistfights. I have come to learn that the elders' collective philosophy is that children have the right to enjoy themselves. 'After all', Grandmother often likes to say, 'as we watch the children caper about, we remember, with throbbing nostalgia, the carefree days of our youth.' When I see tears in her old eyes, I turn away in sadness.

After the colonial days were long over, and independence, and now neo-colonialism, had penetrated to the remotest regions of our country, Mirema acquired a new status as a County; supposed to bring services closer to the people, but we are yet to see these promised services. One thing I am certain about is that our centre, *MiremaOfficiallyMatopeni*, has outgrown itself. It is an oversized slum teaming with life, with ubiquitous unplanned odd-shaped stone buildings, mountains of garbage, and ramshackle kiosks made of raggedy cardboard, poles and plastic sheeting or rusty corrugated iron sheets.

The legendary leisurely green village of my grandparents' time is now a dust bowl created by grunting trucks pulling overloaded trailers along the nearby busy highway. There is a constant line of trucks waiting to drive into the weighbridge, a place that brings us constant misery, lung diseases, HIV and AIDS. Paradoxically, it also brings wealth to visionary entrepreneurs who supply all manner of goods to travellers and the rest of us *privileged* to live here.

Time and time again, my grandparents lament that their beloved Mirema died an ignoble death a long time ago. They grieve for the Mirema of their youth, the Mirema of gurgling springs and streams with crystal-clear water that was sweet to drink. They grieve for the greenness of their Mirema, lamenting that garbage has clogged up the streams and that the once crystal-clear water has turned into sickly gooey sludge with a sheen of

10

black oil across its surface. A nasty, stifling smell emanates from it, polluting the entire width and breadth of *MiremaOfficiallyMatopeni*. People constantly complain about nearby factories spewing chemical waste into the streams, but the Government is silent to these complaints and known deaths from the pollution.

I frequently argue with my two grandfathers that they are imagining things and that our urbanized slum, *MiremaOfficiallyMatopeni*, could never have been the verdant place they describe. But over and over again, they repeat that indeed there had been a time when Mirema and its environs flourished with indigenous trees and wild fruit that grew in profusion. They talk of a land teaming with wildlife; a land with lush green grass during the rainy season; a land of burnt yellow ochres and siennas during the dry season. They remember that while herding cattle and goats, they and their playmates ate wild fruit that kept hunger at bay until the evening when they returned home with the animals to find hot, delicious food waiting for them.

As my grandfathers recall the past, their eyes grow misty with nostalgia. Time and time again, their eyes brim with unshed tears and unable to look into their sad old eyes, I turn away to wipe my own tears cruising down my cheeks. They shake their heads, whispering, again and again, that they miss the years of their youth; lamenting that this New World has let them down; that when Independence came, they had looked forward to new changes, challenges, and hope for a bright future, but that instead they continue to see destruction and devastation born of corruption, voracious appetites and greed perpetuated by our leaders.

Even though I feel sad for my grandfathers, I cannot fully comprehend the changes they talk about because I only know the world as it was now, in my lifetime. I know little else. With raw bitterness in her voice, my mother frequently tells me that they were better off when she was a young girl, saying that there was never a day when they went to bed hungry. 'Not like nowadays. How many nights lately have we not gone to bed on empty stomachs? Too many times to count, Kenia,' she laments, viciously kicking a misshapen aluminium pan and sending it flying across the dusty patch of ground in front of our shack. And there, the unfortunate pan will lie undisturbed until a scavenger picks it up to sell to a scrap iron dealer and it will undoubtedly find its way to China, far, far away from home, to enrich others or to return as a new item.

When I sit with Grandmother and ask her what she thinks about life in general, she says, 'life has changed, my child. This world of ours is no longer the world of our youth. When your mother was young, that dusty road that now leads to the shops was nothing more than a path leading to the stream with its clean water. Bit by bit, changes started to take place. Mirema with its gurgling springs and abundance of greenery came to an end when the Government built that highway right through it, as-suring us the highway would bring us great prosperity. Perhaps it has brought prosperity for business people, but for the rest of us it has brought us sheer despair and diseases. Look at that patch of ground. When it rains, it becomes a muddy pool; during the dry season, the man-made dust is unbearable. Smelly filth has choked up the streams. We have no clean water and we are eating pol-luted vegetables grown in sewerage water. What do you think about that, Kenia, my child?' She waits for my answer.

I have no answer to her penetrating question because I neither remember seeing gurgling springs nor drinking water from crystal-clear streams. Sadly, I watch Grand-mother shake her head, an old woman wrapped up in her beautiful past.

I try to imagine what the village looked like a long time ago, but I cannot. *MiremaOfficiallyMatope* as it is now is what I know. I hardly hear the many types of noises or notice the filth and the dust. I hardly hear the clamour of laughing children; the strident voices of people conversing in a multitude of languages; the grunting and screeching of overloaded buses; trucks with their raucous squeaking hydraulic brakes; and matatus with blaring, deafening music. All sorts of smells assail my eager nostrils; smells of frying fish from Kisumu and sometimes Mombasa, freshly roasted maize and cassava, and above all, the pervasive, tantalizing smell of roasted meat – goat, beef, chicken, and even donkey steak when sly butchers get away with it. All these things are now embedded deep in my psyche. I am an essential part of our semi-urbanized *MiremaOfficiallyMatopeni*, our bustling slum rich with stories and life.

Until I went to the City, I imagined *MiremaOfficiallyMatopeni* to be the only exciting place in our country. The City opened my eyes to another world of wonders. My uncle and my cousin collected me from the terrifying bustling, whirring-twirling country bus terminus. As we drove in their posh car to their home in a leafy, pristine suburb, I stared here and there, my eyes popping out of my tensioned sockets. I saw that every building in sight was a tall gleaming spectacle made even more spectacular by its myriad glinting glass windows. I was afraid the buildings would topple right on top of the car and smother us to death. I cringed and wriggled my body farther back into the seat. The tarmacked roads awed me. The millions of cars whizzing here and there at an incredible speed scared me to death.

Later that evening Uncle drove us to the City for me to see the bright city lights. The neon lights and enormous billboards dazzled and amazed me beyond all imagination. My cousin laughed, teasing me that I was a *real villager*, making sure to emphasize the words. Her snide remarks wounded me, but I was determined not to show the slightest annoyance lest I be sent packing before I had experienced the City to the full.

One morning, my cousin and I went to town alone in a matatu. When we alighted, I stood rooted to the stage, too terrified to cross the busy road. My cousin was already at the other end shouting at me to cross quickly. I run after her and a speeding matatu almost knocked me down. The driver braked, stuck his head out of the window and yelled obscenities at me. My cousin rushed back, grabbed my hand and attempted to drag me across the road. I resisted, unwilling to die before my time. A car braked in front of my faltering steps. I screamed as if all hell had broken loose. I screamed again. Someone in the car yelled, '*mjinga wewe*, do you want to die? *Rudi oshago!*' People stopped in their tracks to stare at me. I felt so humiliated by their abuses, I sobbed, wishing I were back home.

'You are so stupid! Do you want to be killed, you silly fool? How can you be too scared to cross the road? What is your problem?' My cousin yelled, not minding in the least bit that a crowd had quickly gathered around us. She dragged me after her, muttering under her breath about stupid villagers who didn't know how to cross roads and acted just like village sheep.

'Why are you yelling at me? I've never crossed busy city roads with so many lanes and speeding cars,' I retorted tearfully. My heart was racing and pounding so hard, I feared it would explode. Right there and then, I wished I could quickly return to my chaotic but relatively safe *MiremaOfficiallyMatopen*i. When we got home, my cousin told her parents about my stupidity and ineptitude at crossing roads, ending in a cross voice, 'she behaved like a typical villager and embarrassed me! I just hope none of my friends saw us.'

My uncle and aunt merely laughed, assuring me I would soon get used to crossing city roads. And, indeed, I did so in the two weeks I stayed with them. But when it came time to board the bus home, my happiness knew no bounds. I was thrilled to be going home, anticipating the joy of seeing my jacaranda tree and walking along the pot-holed paths of my dust-suffocating but beloved *MiremaOfficiallyMatopeni*.

On the journey back home, I had time to reflect on experiences as a young child growing up in *MiremaOfficiallyMatopeni*. I recalled how my parents changed my name from Kenia to Esther, saying that the teachers recommended pupils to use Christian names at school. My father, a tough stonemason and jack-of-all-trades, vehemently opposed the changing of my name, but my mother and teachers overruled his protests. Back then, it was exciting to have a new name, but in my adulthood, I reverted to Kenia. When people call me Esther I hardly respond because it is alien to me.

With his meagre earnings, my father faithfully paid my primary school fees and religiously saved towards my secondary education, to supplement the Government bursary I would get. My mother saved whatever she could from the little profit she made selling vegetables in a kiosk rented from the council.

I passed my primary exams with good grades and went to a Government boarding school in the City. The boarding school prided itself on its reputation for achieving good results. Soon, from a gawky, shy and tongue-tied village girl, I quickly blossomed into a talkative, vivacious young woman. I often laugh at memories of myself when I first sent to secondary school, recalling embarrassing situations, which had made some of the girls taunt me for being 'backward and a real villager'. During the holidays, I sometimes stayed with my relatives in the city, but preferred returning home to

MiremaOfficiallyMatopeni. Back home, I enthralled my friends with humorous stories about my school life in the City. After my animated talks, practically every girl wanted to go to my school, but they would shrug in a resigned way knowing theirs were wishful hopes because their parents were unable to afford fees for secondary education. My friends' dashed hopes made me frustrated and angry. I resented the sight of young boys and girls loitering at the trading centres with no hope for further education. Bitterness rankled deep within me at the Government's failure to provide free secondary education and instead giving them futile promises that they would *soon* receive training, further education, and even employment; just to be patient.

When I expressed my pain and anger to my father, he said in an equally bitter voice, 'Kenia, complete your studies and go abroad for further studies. There is no future for you here. I want you to go to America for further studies. Your Uncle lives in America and has a Greencard. He has promised to sponsor you to go over there. All he requires is that you work extremely hard and score high grades. If you succeed, you will be of help to all of us here. We cannot wallow in poverty all our lives. What exactly are you interested in studying at University level?'

I gazed around the dusty village and across at the treeless hills where illegal logging had been going on for decades. I looked at the choked up stream, at the decaying filth all around us. I stared at the plastic bags littering every available space of our surroundings. Firmly, resolutely, I said, 'I want to study environmental law,' I had already discussed my career choice with my teachers and they had recommended useful websites for me to check on this choice. I had learned a lot already.

My father tried to persuade me that I should study medicine, stressing the fact that there were too few doctors in our community and that with devolution more doctors would be needed at the county level. He pointed out the health problems facing our village, pointing out that my high grades in school were evidence that I would pass Form Four with flying colours. 'Kenia, you have the intelligence to make an excellent doctor,' Father said emphatically.

At night, I mulled over whatever Father had said, but as far as my career choice was concerned, I was determined to do environmental law. Later in school, I weighed my options with my teachers, but they encouraged me to pursue my idea, agreeing with me that our country needed more lawyers focusing specifically on environmental issues to help safeguard our natural resources and overall environment. When I returned to school each term, my friends remarked that I always returned a changed, a sombre, thoughtful girl.

'Each time you return, you are more withdrawn, impatient, and before we know it, you are so wrapped up in your books we dare not talk to you,' complained Helen, one of my closest friends. 'If you continue to screw up your face in that angry manner, you will turn ugly! Kenia, what is eating you up?'

'Helen, you don't know the hardships of the village or the slums. Going home isn't a holiday for me. I have many chores to perform. Many of my friends are loitering aimlessly in the trading centres with no hope of further education. People are suffering unbelievable hardships despite having a Government. Why should children and the youth lack education? Why should we lack basic amenities like running water and electricity? Helen, you were born and brought up in the city. You have running water and electricity. You have no clue about the hardships of the village. '

'Hey, don't imagine that because I live in the city I know nothing about village life. Don't forget my grandparents live in the village. When I visit them, I help them fetch water and collect firewood. I have experienced hardships, my dear! Actually, most of us in this school know the harsh realities of village life. The person I feel most sorry for is Amina. From all she tells us, she comes from the worst place on earth,' said Helen.

'Even if it is the worst place on earth, it is still home,' said Amina defensively, but with a tinge of underlying anger.

I had to agree with Helen that after listening to Amina's stories about her village in the remote, almost inaccessible Northeastern part of our country, it sounded like a Martian outpost. Her descriptions of Turkana's unforgiving arid and rocky landscape made me appreciate my dusty village. Although I was concerned about Amina's hardships, I was more worried about her eldest sister Rukia who had long ago run away with an elderly German man to Hamburg. They had met whilst he was on safari in Turkana and promised to turn her into a world class model once in Germany. Photographs of her showed she was a beautiful girl who fitted the stereotypical image of a model. For a strictly brought-up Borana girl, it was unbelievable that Rukia had actually run away with a foreigner, an old *mzungu* at that!

Sometime ago, Amina had confided in me that she feared for her sister's life. 'It is now several years since Rukia run away. At first, she used to send me interesting emails full of excitement and descriptions of her new life in Hamburg, but the tone of the emails began to change from excitement to pain and anguish. Last year, she stopped emailing altogether. Several times, my father asked the Ministry of Foreign Affairs to help search for her in Hamburg, but they kept making excuses that since she hadn't registered at the Kenyan embassy, it was difficult to trace her, but that they would look into it. Until now, they have done nothing to find my sister. Rukia thought she was leaving our hellhole of a village for a better life in Europe, but it was all an illusion. For all we know, she could be dead,' said Amina.

Several months back, Amina had shown me a sorrowful email written by Rukia more than a year ago. She had written that she missed the heat and the dust of home, even the fine gritty sand that got into everything and made one's eyes itch horribly. She remembered the rough camel rides and the occasional lorry ride to the nearest trading centres. The email ended with a series of despondent questions. 'Sister, do you dare ask me if I can truthfully miss that desert hellhole where children and people die of hunger, where there are no medical clinics, where there's no water and where the Government doesn't give a damn? Will you dare ask me if I truly miss that godforsaken hellhole? Yes, yes, yes, I miss it terribly, terribly, terribly. Sister, my life here in Hamburg is a living hell. I am Heinrich's slave. He has hidden my passport and doesn't allow me to leave the house unless he accompanies me. Instead of making me into a world-class model, he has turned me into a world-class prostitute. Amina, my dearest sister, I realize I am one of the many women trafficked as prostitutes. I am a captive in a foreign land. One of his friends has promised to help me to get back home. I have no idea if the man is telling me the truth or if he wants to use me like Heinrich. I can only use the computer when Heinrich is drunk and fast asleep. He will surely kill me if he ever finds out I email you. Pray for me. Rukia.'

As I read the email, Amina gave a heart-rending sigh and sobbed uncontrollably. Her sobs shredded my heart. The deep rage burning within me erupted. Between clenched teeth, I asked angrily, 'why should people be lured to seek greener pastures in foreign countries because our Government fails to give them education, fails to enable them find employment, fails to avail medical facilities and basic amenities? What kind of Government abandons its own people? Why should crooks traffic people and turn them into prostitutes and hostages in foreign lands?' I was so angry I didn't realize I was yelling until Amina brought my yelling to a stop by grabbing me and clapping her hand over my mouth. When I had quietened down, she stated loudly and emphatically, 'I am determined to go into politics as soon as I complete University. I am going to start right away by joining the youth forum. One day, I will become a Member of Parliament and once there, I shall fight to make sure my forgotten village gets its rightful share of the national cake. I shall fight for our rights.'

Right there and then, we both made a pledge that from henceforth we would demand our rights at all levels of society. We would fight from the grass-root level to Parliament itself to safeguard our heritage and inalienable rights. We would study hard to achieve good grades to enable us enter University. We would enlighten ourselves on our constitutional and human rights.

One morning, after I had completed my Form Four exams, I woke up to discover someone with a power saw had cut down *my tree*, my beautiful straggly jacaranda to make way for a shop. I stared at the sap, the tree's life force, oozing from the stump. I sat down, wrapped my arms around the tree stump and wept bitterly. People rushed to console me, but I was inconsolable. They were equally angry at the wanton destruction of the tree, but I knew they couldn't fully comprehend the deep pain searing my heart. An unthinking person asked if I had gone insane, asking loudly why I was clinging to the stump of the tree and wailing like a fool. Someone ran to fetch my mother. She arrived panting, shooed away the inquisitive neighbours and tried to comfort me by reminding me that the jacaranda seeds I had planted were already sprouting and would soon grow to be big trees.

As I continued to cling to the oozing stump, right at that precise moment, I made up my mind that I would never leave my country to go to America or Europe or the Far East for further studies. I would study at one of the local universities and during the holidays volunteer in a law firm or NGO fighting for the rights of people and the environment. I made a solemn vow to myself that I would never cease fighting for the rights of my people; never cease fighting for my own rights; never cease fighting to reclaim our country from greedy leaders bent on destroying our future and the future of our children. I would fight to save the flora and fauna of my country. I would be the voice for the voiceless trees, flowers, shrubs, grass, insects, and animals of our country. I would fight for their right to exist. I would do it in memory of my beloved jacaranda tree whose blossoms had given me so much joy and hope throughout my young life.

Later that day, a bulldozer and a truck arrived. The bulldozer dug up the weeping stump with its roots and lifted it onto a waiting truck together with its hacked-off branches and stem cut into even-sized logs. Tearfully, I watched the truck drive away, with *my tree's* roots seeming to wave goodbye to all the bystanders. Quickly, people catered away the shavings, bits and pieces of the stem and sizeable branches for firewood.

Some months after my jacaranda tree had been hacked to death, I discovered that one of the seedlings I had planted ages back had grown into a three foot sapling. I was astonished that all along I had failed to see the seed sprout and the little sapling become erect and strong. I sat next to it and wept quietly, whispering to the brave little sapling that I would protect it until it grew into a vigorous tree like the one whose mauve-blue blossoms had given me so much pleasure and optimism throughout the years of my youth. I can swear I heard it promise me it would grow into a sturdy tree and provide us with welcome shade all year round and, during the seasons of the jacarandas, bring forth amazing mauve-blue blossoms just to please me.

CHAPTER TWO

Ruth

Each night, the two leave me screaming, writhing agonizingly, and covered with streams of sticky sweat. The first one is less terrifying than the second. It is a living, breathing scarecrow, seven feet tall, composed of hordes of hawks with razor-sharp talons, cruel beaks, and glinting eyes. The monstrous scarecrow, with its vicious eyes focused on me, dives speedily, and grips me tightly with its powerful claws. It begins to peck me slowly at first and then ravenously, shredding me into bloody strips. It claws me mercilessly, until blood runs down my head, my face, my neck, and to my arms and hands. Struggling out of its stranglehold, I fall facedown to the ground, thrashing about in indescribable agony. My blood saturates the ground. A mixture of blood and mud floods my mouth. The muck chokes me. Sensing I am dying, I beseech God to save me, but all I hear is the deafening screeching of the monstrous scarecrow advancing towards me with its hundreds of cruel beaks and talons outstretched with menacing intent.

Swiftly, it dives on me, picks me up with its powerful talons and impales me into the sharpened barbs of a wire fence. I dangle helplessly. Methodically, it rips the rest of my body into minute strips with its myriads of sharpened talons. With merciless intent, it feasts on my head, on my bleeding face, and on my neck. I ask God to shield my eyes; beseech Him to throw a protective shroud over me, but all I hear is the fiendish shriek of the scarecrow. I want to shield my face, but I can't move my shredded hands. I beseech God to answer my prayers, begging Him to allow me to die quickly. Turning my face upward, I see the second monstrosity dive towards me.

Mesmerized, I watch it dive slowly – slowly – slowly –slowly - silently – silently - silently towards me. It is more terrifying than the first. It is a grotesque flying beast made up of a multitude of vicious butcherbirds protruding from all sides of its body. More butcherbirds protrude from its ugly misshapen head. The beast suddenly picks up speed and dives with lightning speed. It pounces on weaker birds and impales them into the sharpened spikes of the barbed wire fence. The butcherbirds erupt from the terrible form and begin to ferociously shred the pitiful birds into tiny bloody morsels, greedily swallowing the pieces without pausing. I wonder how such innocent-looking birds, with glistening black and white plumage, can be so merciless, so rapacious. I shudder in disbelief at such insatiable cruelty.

As I continue to watch, from all directions, thousands of hawks and vultures join in the feast, shoving the butcherbirds aside. Calculatingly, they fight over the bloody bodies of the little birds, gorging themselves until their bloated bodies are at bursting point. Realizing I am their next victim, I shut my bloody eyes; wriggle my tortured body into a tight ball on the ground, waiting for inevitable, final death. The hawks and vultures advance towards me and begin to tear me apart with their brutal beaks and talons. The pain is unbearable. Again and again, I scream piercingly until my head explodes, spilling out all my brains, which splatter on the ground like spaghetti. I know that within seconds, I will be surely dead. I beseech God, yet again, to come to my aid, but all I hear is the horrifying, piercing shrieks of butcherbirds, hawks, and vultures. I know I will die quickly. How long will God remain silent? How long? I weep bitterly.

No amount of counselling has been able to rid my mind of these merciless monsters. They are always there, deep, deep in my mind, each night torturing me in quick succession. Yet, even though I know I have been clawed and pecked to death, somehow I waken from death. When I open my eyes, I hear two other spectres commanding me to do their bidding. One implores me to recall *something important*, while the other commands me to *forget everything*. I toss and turn, toss and turn, my mind a mass of swirling thoughts – some spiralling helter-skelter, some truncated, some elongated, some incoherent, and always petrifying. In the throes of my anguish, I ask frantically, '*remember what? Forget what? What do you want me to remember or to forget*? I struggle to sit up but collapse back on a surface embedded with sharpened nails which brutally pierce right through my raw back. The pain is unbearable. I scream, but the harder I scream, the deeper the nails penetrate my back until their blood-covered tips emerge from my belly and chest. I shout for help but my voice is too feeble and no one comes to my aid. Instead, I see the same hordes of butcherbirds, hawks and vultures surround me, their cruel beaks and glinting talons outstretched towards me. I hear their shrieks of victory as they swoop down on me. I shut my eyes tightly – tightly - tightly, averting my eyes from their horrifying gleaming ones. I recall that they had already killed me. An incongruous thought stirs my mind; I wonder why God refuses to answer my pleas, yet I pay tithes faithfully. How many times will I die and be reborn?

Piercing pain shoots from my toes, through my spine to my head. I need to concentrate my scattered thoughts into meaningful coherence, but someone is driving a spear with a lethal tip into my skull. I clench my fists, grit my teeth, and plead desperately, '*stop torturing me! God, help me!*' The spear penetrates deeper into my skull until a stream of warm liquid trickles down my face. The trickle continues into my half-opened mouth. The taste of my own blood is disgusting. I try to spit it out, but it clings tightly to the walls of my mouth, nauseating me. I know if I don't spit it out, it will choke me to death. '*God, help me! Please help me!*' I beg, turning my neck from side to side.

Deep in my mind, a strident voice commands me in a jarring singsong staccato voice to '*remember! Forget! Remember! Forget!*' But just as quickly, another voice orders, '*forget everything. I forbid you to remember anything!*' I taste more blood in my mouth. It is salty and revolting. Finally, I manage to spit some out, but in doing so, the trickle becomes a steady rivulet until I know I am drowning in my own repellent blood. I wonder how long it will take me to die a second time; or is it the third or fourth or fifth time? I wonder how I came back to life.

Hot tears of panic prick my eyes. I struggle to sit up, but the sharpened nails have permanently pinned me to the cruel surface. I writhe in agony, unable to spit out the blood flooding my mouth. I wonder where all the blood is coming from. My question is followed by a scorching fire which sets my head ablaze with such intensity, I want to rip my head off my shoulders and fling it to the farthest corners of the earth. My head is splitting. I shut my eyes tightly until I see millions of dazzling stars dancing around me; millions of razor-sharp rotary drills boring into my skull. Scalding blood streams from my eyes into my open mouth and I realize I am weeping tears of blood. I beg someone to take away the excruciating pain, but all I hear is killing silence; deadly silence followed by the mocking laughter of butcherbirds and hawks. I cringe in terror as they advance towards me, frenziedly flapping their lethal wings. I pray to die before they claw me to death. My prayer is answered. I float away, far away into a tunnel of enveloping soft, cushioning blackness. I float far away from the cruel flying monsters.

In death, I am secure, wrapped in the warmth of spongy blackness which cradles me in its arms, singing me my favourite lullaby; rocking me gently in perfect rhythm. Abruptly, magically, miraculously, the indescribable pain shooting through my tortured boy dissipates. My mind becomes crystal-clear. I look into a crystal ball and see every microscopic detail of my life unfold before my focused eyes. In my security, I piece my life together, unravelling details and fragments of my shattered being. But just at the precise moment of revelation, I see an amorphous apparition emerge from the crystal ball and take shape, becoming a captivating young woman pirouetting joyfully, tantalizingly before my glazed eyes. I recognize the enchanting woman as Melpomene who has come to resurrect me. With a click of her finger, she restores me to life. She floats before my eyes, dancing enticingly, inviting me to cavort with her, urging me to remember *something important.* I promise to recollect whatever it is she wants me to recall. Smiling gently, she lovingly pats my face, telling me not to be afraid. I weep in relief that she has come to my rescue. But because I am afraid of her, I cajole my mind to remember *something important.* My obedient mind obeys me and I quickly begin to piece the fragments together.

But, as the fragments coalesce and take shape, to my horror, Melpomene transforms into s stern-faced demon I recognize as Mwangamizi. The demon commands me to *deny everything, to forget everything,* in fact to *destroy every single memory* I have. It dances around me, spinning at such a speed that my head rotates uncontrollably. Imperiously, Mwangamizi beckons me to follow it. When I try to, I find that it has bound my legs with unbreakable steel chains. It laughs mockingly, taunting

27

me to break the chains. In desperation, I weep because, no matter how hard I try, I can't break the metal chains. How long will the demon torture me?

Before I can answer my own question, Mwangamizi transforms back to Melpomene, a tender, loving being, full of songs, laughter, and comforting words. In the clarity of my mind, I am suddenly eager to listen to Melpomene's soothing whispers and hypnotic tunes. I beg her to come closer and reveal her secrets or her commands. I pledge to obey all her instructions. She leans closer, whispering softly into my alert ears, saying, '*I will help you to remember because I am finite – everlasting - forever.*' She beckons me to follow her deep into the past. She commands me to recite after her, '*I am an African-American who will forever recall gleaming chains and shackles around my tortured body. I will forever recall the stench – the filth – the cruelty of slave ships. I will forever feel the torturing pain of red-hot branding irons, which my successive slave masters, imprinted their claim over me as their possession and beast of burden. I will forever hear the anguished lamentations of my fellow slaves.*' Incoherent images form in my mind. I am unable to recite all her words. I tremble with anger at Melpomene for taking me to a world in which I do not belong. Insisting loudly, Melpomene commands me to recite her lines.

When I stumble to the end of my incoherent recital, Melpomene urges me to intone, '*I am a Jew who will forever recall the Holocaust. I am an African freedom fighter who defied millions of bullets to bring liberation to our people.*' When I remain silent, her gentle whispers suddenly became booming, angry ones. Her angry words are so loud my ears feel as if they will explode. I struggle to comprehend her words and when I cannot, I become extremely angry again, ordering her to vacate my mind, but she commands me to recite her words. I weep in anguish because I don't understand why she is thrusting me into history that is not mine. Her furious whispers become cruel spears puncturing my eardrums. In desperation, I promise to obey her, straining my ears for her next orders, but my head becomes so heavy, all I want to do is to sleep forever. I close my eyes tightly, refusing to look at Melpomene, and wish for death again. She gives me a hard slap me to waken me, tilting my face until her eyes bore into mine. Her eyes are violet blue.

In a gentle, lilting voice, she says, *'I am in your deepest psyche, in your DNA. Before you were born, your DNA already contained collective memories. You cannot flee from me. You are my eternal prisoner. If you want me to free you, you must remember something important!'* Her soft murmurs suffuse my entire being. *'What I am supposed to remember*?'I ask. In an authoritative voice, she tells me that it is imperative for me to remember *something, anything, everything* - the emphasis on each word is unmistakable. In frustration, I weep more tears of blood, asking her why she is torturing me. She forces me to look at something she is pointing at. I focus hard and see before my eyes a gigantic mirror shimmering with kaleidoscopic fragments. The mirror fills the entire space of my mind. Soon, the scintillating fragments fall into place and begin to take shape. Suddenly, a full image pops out at me. It is of me, but instead of my being beautiful, I am horribly distorted with indistinguishable features. My face is terribly scarred and my body in bloody tatters. Frantically, I break the mirror into minute, unrecognizable pieces. Melpomene shakes her head angrily. I tremble at her evident rage. I know I have to flee from her before she kills me. I know I have to because I see her aiming a sharpened spear at me.

But she grabs me by my neck, pulling me upwards until I am hovering in the sky. Pointing downwards, she urges me to look, but I resist because I am terrified of heights. She holds me firmly, forcing my face downwards. There below us, I see myself lying on the ground. I am saturated in mud and blood. I see thousands of butcherbirds, hawks, and vultures converge on me. Frighteningly, the birds turn into youths in their early twenties, my own age, and others even younger. They punch me in the face, throw me to the ground, viciously kick me in the stomach and then repeatedly, mercilessly, stab me with their sharpened spears. They stuff my mouth with a filthy mixture of blood and mud so that I am unable to shout for help. One by one, they rape me - again and again - and again- and again – and again, until I am a mangled heap of bloody flesh, writhing on the ground in unimaginable pain. Still hovering in the sky, I gaze down on my distorted, bedraggled, shredded body enveloped in mud and blood. Closing my eyes tightly, I shudder in horror, but Melpomene forces them open, commanding me to look downwards.

I see a youth bludgeon my mother to death with a lethal knob-ended club made from hardwood. Her skull splits open, spouting an upward stream of blood. I hear myself screaming for help. Unable to stand the terrible sight, I struggle out of Melpomene's grip, but she commands me to look at the houses and granaries, full of recent harvests, go up in smoke. Our house and granary are on fire. Thick grey smoke engulfs everything. Melpomene rotates me slowly and I observe that the whole country is on fire. I hear incessant gunshots and exploding teargas canisters. I see thousands of dead bodies; bodies burned beyond recognition; thousands of mutilated bodies; hundreds of severed limbs scattered here and there. I hear agonized lamentations of thousands of people. Shuddering in terror, I clap my hands to my ears to shut out the lamentations. I close my eyes to shut out the dreadful images, but Melpomene prises them open. I see a dishevelled, sobbing eight-year-old girl pull me into a grove of eucalyptus saplings. I am heavy, but bit by bit she pulls me into the grove. I beg Melpomene to give me respite, to have pity on me. She relents, taking me back down to earth slowly. She allows me to fall asleep.

But as I drop off to sleep, Mwangamizi returns, insisting on possessing me entirely. I manage to push the demon out of my mind. It disappears. I strain my ears for the twitter of my beloved weaverbirds. I wonder why there is no twitter of weaverbirds in our jacaranda tree whose canopy provides welcome shade in our garden. I hear the stealthy steps of Mwangamizi coming towards me. I am deadly afraid it will return and explode my ears into searing fragments with its penetrating, reverberating voice. I am afraid it will inflict unbearable pain on me. Strangled sounds erupt from my mouth. I shout piercingly, '*go away! I want nothing to do with you. Leave me alone*!' Miraculously, it obeys, disappearing into nothingness.

In Mwangamizi's place stands my beloved tall, athletic boyfriend Charlie with his perpetually smiling gentle face. He stretches out his arms to embrace me. I engulf him in a bear hug, weeping in relief that he has come to my rescue. In his arms, I feel overwhelmingly protected. Over and over again, I kiss him. He returns my kisses and his kisses become delicious strawberries. I eat them hungrily. He leads me to a sofa, sits down, lifts me onto his lap and wraps his arms around me. In the safety of his loving arms, I begin to fall asleep, but Mwangamizi erupts before us, pushing Charlie violently away. It throws a red-hot cauldron at me. The cauldron breaks, releasing thousands of demons that want to kill me. Summoning all my strength, I ask Charlie to chase away the advancing demons, but Mwangamizi grabs hold of him and cracks open his skull with a club. Charlie falls to the ground, blood spouting from his skull. I beg someone to save Charlie. No one comes to his aid. I cry out, '*Grandmother, help us!*' Even though I know Grandmother died years ago, I repeat, *Grandmother, help us!*'

Miraculously, my desperate cries bring Grandmother running to my side. She wraps me in her warm, velvety black mantle, soaking up all my sorrows and anguish, gently massaging my mutilated body, easing away the needle-hot, searing shafts of agony. She sings me a lullaby imploring me to sleep. I beg her to save Charlie and Mother. She promises she will save them. Her lullaby soothes me. As I gaze at beloved Grandmother, she disappears without warning. Left alone, I become deadly afraid. I hear more anguished cries, reverberating lamentations that sweep across the nation. A voice tells me the cries are the dirges of thousands of people. I scream for Grandmother. She returns, gathers my quivering body to her bosom, and sings me another lullaby. Warm and secure in her arms, I try to sleep, but she beseeches me to resist sleep until I have ejected the terrible images out of my mind, gently whispering that I must expel them before they completely annihilate me. I tell Grandmother I will obey her. She transforms into Melpomene. I tremble in fear.

I close my eyes, searching for youths, hawks, and butcherbirds in the deepest recesses of my mind in order to eject them. I focus all my energies on finding these lurking demons with their cruel weapons, talons and beaks, waiting to shred me again and again into tiny strips of raw flesh. Someone needs to help me chase away these merciless monsters. Horrible images flash before my eyes - my mother and Charlie bludgeoned to death – me tattered and bleeding – people without limbs, dead children and mutilated adults. I beg for help, desperate to hear assuring human voices. No one comes to my aid, not even my beloved grandmother, not even

Melpomene. All around me is silence. But the silence is as soft as fallen jacaranda blossoms. Images of jacaranda trees float before my eyes. I focus on their mauve-blue perfection. Soon, I fall into deep slumber.

Hours later, I wake up. Someone is forcing water into my parched mouth. I lick my cracked lips slowly and then thirstily. More water dribbles into my mouth. I gag and vomit. Someone wipes my mouth, whispering soothing words into my ears. I attempt to open my eyes, but they are tightly gummed to my eyelids. It is too painful to open them. The murmuring voice urges me to drink more water. I turn away, wondering why the person is unable to comprehend that I don't want any more water. The person prises my mouth open, forcing water into it. I gulp and swallow. The water is cool against the parched walls of my mouth. Suddenly, I want more water. 'Water, water,' I whisper. Tiny trickles enter my mouth, soothing my burning throat. The water gradually awakens me. Little by little, I force my eyes open, but I see nothing but thick white fog. I need to rub my eyes, but I can't move my arms. 'I am in so much pain,' I say aloud, startling myself at my rasping voice. Someone pops a capsule and water into my mouth. This time I don't gag. I swallow the pill and the water. In a few minutes, the intense pain throughout my body begins to subside. I lie back against a pillow propped behind my head. Amazingly, my mind becomes lucid. As clear as day, I recollect all that had taken place.

I am in the midst of that particular day; in the present moment, in the *now*. The weather is sweltering hot. So oppressively hot that my skin tightens, an overstretched drum ready to burst. The air is dense, humid, stifling, and stagnant. Everything is motionless; not a leaf moves, not a blade of grass sways. There is no twitter of weaverbirds in the branches of the acacia and jacaranda trees. Overhead, the sky is a dazzling, fiery blue tinged with purple, reminding me of jacaranda blossoms with their ever-changing mauve-blues. Intermittent mirages skim over recently harvested maize fields, glide over stacks of maize, and shimmer out of sight. Spiralling dust devils soon follow; huge tunnels of dusty air filled with all manner of flying rubbish. '*The calm before the storm,*' I tell myself. As this thought flits through my mind, grey, angry clouds swirl out of nowhere, obscuring the sun. '*Sure signs of a storm,*' I say aloud, imagining the swirling clouds as frenzied dancers teasing the sun. I smile at the unexpected image in my mind. '*How I hate storms!*' I say, shivering despite the sweltering heat.

A sudden gust of wind rips through the nearby eucalyptus saplings, bending branches until they almost touch the ground. Weaverbirds dart out of their duplex nests. Dust devils whip up dust, leaves, and scraps of rubbish and swirl them high into the sky. As the dust devils whirl out of sight, I look upwards, shading my eyes against a sudden flash of lightning. Successive bolts of lightning streak across the darkening sky. Rumbling thunder sounds from afar, gradually getting louder. A piercing clap of thunder makes me hastily block my ears with my fingers. I quiver in dread, having never lost my childhood fear of reverberating thunder, but thankful that such tropical storms are usually short-lived. 'At least, the rain will lessen this oppressive January heat,' I say aloud. As I turn to go inside the house, I hear strident voices in the distance, as if a thousand football fans are spurring on their favourite teams. I strain my ears to determine the direction of the rowdy voices. In the distance, I see people milling around as if a skirmish has begun. I call out in a very loud, anxious voice, 'Mum, it's about to rain and there is a lot of noise coming from the direction of the polling centre. I wonder what's happening over there.' I hear sporadic gunshots and the sound of exploding teargas canisters. I quiver in alarm.

My mother steps out of the house and she too gazes at the darkening sky. 'I'm glad it's going to rain. This oppressive heat is killing me. Ruth, do you hear gunshots? I hope there isn't any trouble at the polling centre.' I see my mother visibly tremble as we watch spirals of smoke snake skywards. 'Something is definitely wrong, Ruth. Perhaps there is trouble at the centre. What might be the cause of those spirals of smoke? I hope Patrick isn't in that crowd.' There is rising trepidation in my mother's voice and more tremors shoot through her body. No doubt, she is worried about Patrick, her intrepid son and my brother who left several hours ago to cast his vote. Mum and I left home at four in the morning, had waited patiently for the centre to open, had cast our votes and returned home for a welcome cup of milky tea and chunks of white bread.

We watch group of youths come from the direction of the polling centre at a run towards us. We hear more bursts of gunshots and exploding teargas canisters. In dread, I say, 'Mum, those youths are heading this way. Perhaps the anti-riot police are chasing them.' I remember the many times I had been caught up in riots at the university and the suffocating tear gas that burned eyes with red-hot pepper fumes. Suddenly, my mother grabs me by the arm. 'Ruth, those boys are brandishing weapons!' I break out in cold shivers at the sight of the advancing youths, some wielding glinting machetes and others brandishing thick branches. There are no riot police behind them. As we stare keenly at the advancing youths, my boyfriend's eight-year-old sister Mercy comes sprinting towards us. She hurls herself at me and clings tightly to me, sobbing hysterically.

'What's the matter, Mercy?' I ask, holding the scruffy child at arm's length. Even though Mercy is not my sister, sisterly love for her saturates my body especially because she is my boyfriend Charlie's sister. I had discovered that whenever Mercy trots loyally by my side to the nearby trading centre, loitering youths rarely accost me with their lurid words and flirtatious innuendoes. But whenever I go alone, the idle boys predictably confront me, laughing hilariously at my apparent discomfort and seething annoyance. I shake Mercy almost violently. 'Tell us why you are crying, Mercy.' She tells us that boys have burnt their house and beaten her mother until she was bleeding. Mercy wails even louder. My mother pulls her to her side protectingly. I watch apprehensively as the rowdy youths come tearing along the path, setting alight two of the neighbours' homes and granaries. Sensing imminent danger, I look at my mother in trepidation. She grabs hold of Mercy's hand and runs towards the eucalyptus saplings. 'Run, Mercy, run!' They stumble and fall.

A strident voice yells, 'don't let them get away!' before I can make a move, a burly youth grabs hold of me, flings me to the ground and viciously kicks me. From the corner of my eye, I see my mother pick herself up and advance towards the youth, yelling, 'leave my daughter alone!' I spring to my feet in time to see a youth land a blow across her skull with a club. She reels and falls to the ground, a jet of blood spurting upwards and streams running down the side of her head. I let out a horrified scream. I run to my mother's side. Blood is streaming from her cracked skull. Her body is twitching horribly. I hear myself screaming- screaming- screaming. I recognize the youth. 'Martin! What are you doing? I clutch his arm. 'Martin, what have you done? Oh, my God, you have killed my mother!' I scream, shaking him violently.

Belligerently, he stares back at me with blood-red eyes, a sure sign he has smoked plenty of *bhangi*. He grabs me by the neck and gives me a stinging slap. 'Stop that bloody screaming and take a good look at this traitor. Admit in front of all of us that you know him well.'

He pulls me towards my boyfriend Charlie whose face shows he has been thoroughly beaten up. When I do not respond, Martin viciously kicks my shins. 'Admit you know this traitor, your-so-called boyfriend!' When I still do not respond, he gives me a resounding slap. 'If you don't reply, I'll crack open your skull the same way I did your mother's!' Shuddering in terror, I say, 'yes, that is Charlie, my boyfriend.' I begin to wail loudly. Martin yanks me by the neck and shoves my face into Charlie's. 'Take a last look at your so-called boyfriend before we finish him off. Charlie, you traitor, if you are a real man, rape her in front of all of us.' With a repulsive expression on his face, Martin turns to me and says, 'today, your boyfriend and the rest of us will teach you a lesson you will never forget. Charlie, stand up do your job or else I will finish you off!' He pushes me towards Charlie who clenches his fists, ready to strike Martin, yelling that Martin would have to kill him because he would never rape me.

Martin moves closer to Charlie. 'If you hit me, you will regret it, you bastard. And if you don't rape her, your ultimate punishment will not be death but castration, you bastard!' He spits straight into Charlie's face, smacking his fist into Charlie's swollen eyes. 'Rape her now!'

Charlie staggers from the blow, but quickly straightens up. 'I will never rape my girlfriend! You will have to kill me or castrate me, because I will never rape her.'

I watch Charlie summon all the strength he can muster. He aims a blow at Martin, but Martin sidesteps him and clobbers him on the side of his head with a club. Charlie falls to the ground. I run to his side and lean over him begging him to stand up. Martin pulls me away, holding me with an iron grip. With his right hand, he punches me in the face, bellowing hatefully that he is going to teach me a lesson, that I am an arrogant University bitch. He tells the youths he will be the first to rape me and after he is done, they can all take a turn; that I am his gift to them; that they can claim to have had sex with a University girl. Trembling in terror, I watch the youths wave their gleaming machetes in the air and advance towards me. They break out in raucous, demonic laughter. They all bear the telltale marks of alcohol and *bhangi.*

Martin calls out to William, a student with us at the University. He came to my twenty-first birthday a month ago and even brought me a box of chocolates. 'William, drag away this half-dead traitor to our base. Later on, we will castrate him for sleeping with our enemies.' Helplessly, I watch as William and another youth drag away Charlie.

Martin steps close to me. There is hate in his eyes and in his voice. He says viciously, 'all along you thought Charlie was the only man for you, didn't you? All along, you considered me beneath you, didn't you? Now, I will teach you a lesson you will never forget, you University prostitute!' He puts down his club and quickly unzips his jeans. Before I can take a step, he throws me violently to the ground. I jump up, but he grabs me by the neck, slaps me very hard, pulls my face close to his, and dares me to try it again.

I gaze at him with beseeching eyes. 'What have I ever done to you, Martin? Why do you want to brutalize me?' Struggling in vain to get out of his grip, I yell at the top of my voice, 'somebody, help me! Help me! I look towards the grove of eucalyptus saplings and see Mercy crouching behind them. I pray she runs away before the youths see her and molest her.

Martin throws me to the ground yelling, 'shout all you want, there is no one to come to your aid,' He kicks me savagely in the stomach. I scream in pain. 'The rest of you, when I am done with her, you can all take a turn. She is my gift to you. Set the house and granary on fire.' Instructing two youths to pin me to the ground, Martin tears off my jeans. He rapes mercilessly, brutally, repeatedly. The shame and degrading of my being is far, far more excruciating than my physical pain. Soon, I am unable to move. I am choking to death with my saliva mixed with dirt. Finally, Martin gets off me, urging the others to follow suit, roaring at the slowness of their pace. One by one, the youths rape me. They are vicious, ruthless, inhuman beings. None of them seems to remember he has a grandmother, a mother, a sister, an aunt. At last, they run off, shrieking triumphantly like football revellers who had just won a trophy, leaving behind mayhem.

I thrash about in excruciating pain. Like Jesus, I cry out agonizingly, '*My God, my God, why have you forsaken me?*' But God is silent. I struggle to get up but I cannot move my body. In my mind, I beg little Mercy for water to quench my thirst, to cool my parched throat, to assuage my burning body, to soothe my seared insides. Summoning all the power within me, I whisper, 'Mercy, Mercy, help me!' The next minute, I feel her dragging me, telling me we have to hide in the nearby eucalyptus grove. I know I am much too heavy for her, but bit by bit she drags me along, pausing now and then to get a better grip of me. I hear her heart-rending sobs.

Finally, I am lying under the shade of the eucalyptus saplings. Mercy's little soft hands wipe the blood off my face. I want to scream for help, but I have no strength. I writhe on the ground, begging Mercy to give me water. I hear her running off. Afraid that she will not return, I try to shout for her to come back, but my voice is a mere croak. After a while, Mercy holds a cracked tin cup of water to my mouth. I sip some but feel the rest run down my neck. I implore her to throw cold water on my burning body, wanting to beg her to throw cold water into my *secret parts* to soothe the pain, but I am ashamed for her to see my shredded bloody flesh. I am ashamed that she, a mere child, will see how my private parts have been ripped apart by ruthless rapists. Instead, I ask her for more water to drink and some to pour onto my burning body. I hear her running off. I squirm, praying she will return with the coldest water she can find. This time, I will be brave enough to ask her to throw the water into my raw, shredded secret parts. As if in answer to my pleas, I hear a clap of piercing thunder and then the storm breaks. The rain pelts me, massaging my brutalized body. I drift into enveloping blackness.

Drifting in and out of consciousness, I hear my brother Patrick's alarmed voice calling names. Mercy responds with a shrill cry. Patrick's strident voice jolts me to wakefulness. I feel his arms around me; hear him cry out, 'oh, my God, what have they done to you, Ruth?' I feel him scoop me into his arms, vowing revenge, murder. Tears stream down my face. I whisper to Patrick that I am unable to block out the horrifying lamentations of people, telling him I fear the dirges will make me go deaf. He strokes my face gently, assuring me he will always take care of me. Mercy's pitiful sobs make me weep. I feel guilty because I have no strength to comfort her; no strength to pull her into my arms and soothe away her fears; no voice to thank her for all she has done for me. In desperation, I weep scalding tears. Patrick rocks me gently in his arms. I hear his sobs.

Thick white fog swirls all around me, obscuring Patrick and Mercy. I know I am dying. Beyond the fog, I see friends searching frantically for jacaranda blossoms to make mauve-blue wreaths for my grave. In a strangled whisper, I tell them it isn't yet the season of the jacarandas, that they must wait two more months, but they do not hear me. Grateful for the warm enveloping fog cushioning my tortured being, I close my heavy, gritty eyes. In the distance, I hear lamentations.

CHAPTER THREE

Evelyn

I discovered my real worth in the season of the jacarandas, when the glittering mass of mauve-blue blossoms dazzled against the brilliant blue of the African sky, spinning my head in all directions. In that season, the startling blueness of the bell-shaped blossoms cushioned my pain with their breathtaking loveliness; wrapping my soul and my sorrows within in their glorious wonder; smothering me with protective love; soothing my bleeding heart with their softest touch. In that season, the jacarandas mended my shattered soul, cocooning each fragment of my being within the safety of their arms. In that season of pain, the exquisite blossoms with irrepressible beauty, helped me to untangle my innermost feelings, helped me to unravel myself.

The ever-changing mauve-blues of the blossoms set me free, giving me unbelievable courage to proclaim my name aloud until my lungs reached exploding point. I discovered my love for my name, which I pronounced repeatedly until my voice reverberated beyond the walls of my confinement. 'My name is Eve! My name is Eve! My name is Eve! My name is Evelyn!' My pronouncement became my liberation song, uniting with the bluest blue of the jacarandas to become a pulsating rhythm, each time threatening to explode my constricted heart. I became a living, breathing Eve, breaking free from the enslaving tightly woven cocoon with which I had for so long shrouded my soul. Rising from the ashes of despair and powered by my new wings of liberation, I transformed into a shimmering phoenix ready to fly far away from my prison of desolation.

In that season of the jacarandas, I savoured the sweetness of my name, the sweetness of myself. I had never truly understood the charm of my name until I spoke it aloud in my pain and anguish. 'What is in a name?' I asked aloud as if I were addressing a roomful of people. As if educating myself, I answered that Eve is the shortened version of my baptismal name Evelyn; that some people call me *Lyn*; simply that - no subtlety, no beauty, no melody, no magic to cushion its coldness; usually waiting with bated breath for them to complete it into *lynx* and turn me into an incomprehensible feline she-devil. My relatives prefer *Ever-leen,* spoken in definitive, no nonsense tones as if they are the originators of my name.

When my mother hears this mispronunciation of my name, she laments, always in petulant tones, that my name long ago lost its magical Irishness; as if she, an African woman, is Irish-born or has claim to Irishness, or as if the name is actually Irish. Once, when I questioned her on this, she answered that the Irish nuns who gave me the name had taught her how to pronounce it *properly* and had told her the name is derived from an Irish word for 'radiance' or 'beauty'. I replied that I had read somewhere that the name is derived from a French word for hazelnut, but she adamantly refused to accept my version. Strangely enough, I have to admit that whenever she enunciates my name, she does so with lilting sweetness that leaves me smiling at the incongruity of it all. An African woman with a lilting Irish accent! How bizarre!

My dearest friends call me *Eve*, uttering it with an intonation of love, of oneness, of protectiveness. Their intonation evokes the very Eve-ness of that faraway place where we are made to believe all good things of life existed long before Eve is said to have invented

Original Sin, which led to the unspeakable expulsion from Eden and its Tree of Life laden with goodies and golden promises. On my friends' lips, 'Eve' becomes our collective name, uniting us with our long-ago Garden-of-Eden expelled sister. When my mother's church friends hear this version of my name, they visibly cringe, vehemently protesting in heightened whispers that 'Eve' conjures up images of wicked women offering alluring forbidden fruits to innocent men. Innocent men? Tell me another stupid story!

As for my husband Adam, when we started dating soon after his return from America, he pronounced my name with such tenderness and love it set me all aglow. My friends claimed that they were envious of me whenever they heard Adam say my name. My mother nodded approvingly each time she heard Adam pronounce my name. Until Adam let out the secret that she had coached him, I thought he had learned its proper pronunciation in America.

In that season of my agony, I wondered how Adam's tender pronunciation of my name had been replaced by hateful, grating mispronunciation. Travelling down the path of painfilled memories, I recalled how, at the beginning of our marriage, Adam had proudly shown me off to his colleagues as a rare village girl with – wonders of wonders –a Bachelor of Science degree, soon to embark on a Masters! After our marriage, he indulged me; took me on expensive trips, bought me exquisite gifts, red roses, and assorted Swiss chocolates; an expensive habit he had acquired during his student days in America when his girlfriends expected nothing less on Birthdays and Valentine's. Like a smitten fool, I fell under Adam's magnetic lure into a deep trance - the illusion of grandeur – the illusion of a First Lady. Magazines with beautiful models and prominent women became part of my menu. I went to the gym, applied lotions, bleaching creams, over-the-top make-up, and luscious wigs to transform myself into one of these enviable Venuses with pouting lips and pear-shaped figures. Each day, I waited eagerly to metamorphose into an exquisite butterfly specifically for my beloved Adam. One day, when I looked into my full-length mirror, I beheld a truly gorgeous woman. 'Wow!' I yelled, 'is this really Evelyn that gawky village girl of long ago?' I smiled broadly, happy that my persistence had paid off.

But ten years into our marriage, things began to change imperceptibly. First, Adam's intonation of my name began to bristle with undeniable, contemptuous undercurrents. One day, seemingly from nowhere, a torrent, a deluge, a *tsunami* burst my gigantic rainbow-coloured bubble of complacency. Everything came to a crashing end. My provider became *the* primeval caveman. When he turned primeval, no amount of patient reasoning would convince him I was not *The Original Eve*; that Mythical Woman imbued with extraordinary powers of deception, lust, and Original Sin; that Mythical Woman who entraps men, gobbling up their hard-earned money, guzzling their very essence and existence until they shrivel up and die. To Adam, I became the embodiment of that Evil Woman wickedly enticing him with offerings of forbidden fruit. I was *eating up his money;* conveniently forgetting that I too earned a salary which he insisted must be used for our household expenses. He didn't even allow me to send my parents and siblings a cent of my earnings. Adam's lavish gifts stopped. No more expensive perfumes. No more red roses. No more Swiss chocolates. No more show-off champagne parties. No more gallivanting abroad. No more intimacy. My world crumpled when his wedding band disappeared from his finger.

Time after time, bit by bit, Adam's sneering undercurrents began to plunge me into a churning cauldron of sadness, melancholy, and transient depression which I tried to suppress by slowly but surely wriggling my soul into a tight cocoon, stifling my emotions and my bubbly, happy laughter. I became as dispassionate towards Adam as he was towards me. To my friends, relatives and colleagues, I painted a picture of a habitually happy, fulfilled, and prosperous wife. Sometimes, I heard them whisper that I could never be truly happy and contented because I was childless; that I was simply pretending to be happy. Adam's relatives told me I should allow him to marry a second wife because without children no one would regard him as a *real* man.

Before long, Adam had created an impressive litany of my shortcomings. Laced with alcohol, his raucous, mocking laughter became a daily incantation of the misery I had brought him over the years. 'Evelyn, my dear wife, you have ruined my life – you are the curse of my life – you are eating me alive – you have turned me into a slave! You have eaten my manhood! You are a greedy woman! And on top of it all, you are childless- barren, a desert!' His slurred words took on a strange, almost melodious, rhythm which played in my head, making me slowly rock to its magnetism. Adam would remind me that when he first left for America, I was a shy, ignorant gangly fifteen year old village girl with a hideous shorn head. After a long sip of his favourite cognac, he would burst into laughter. 'You were quite ugly then, weren't you, Evelyn?'

It is true that I was a gawky village girl with a shorn head to keep away lice. From my old photographs, I acknowledge I was not pretty then, but why then had he deigned to date me when he returned from America? I had meet him only once through his sister Sophie. Before he flew away to America, I trooped with other villagers to his home for a befitting send-off feast hosted by his father and a multitude of their clan's people. The next day, he left for the city where he was to take an aeroplane to America the following Friday. Precisely a week later, agape with excitement, all of us villagers turned our eyes skyward, craning our necks to see the aeroplane that was carrying Adam to a faraway land. When a plane appeared high in the sky, we waved frantically, yelling that we could see Adam waving back. Adults openly rejoiced that one of their own had left for further studies abroad.

After Adam's departure, our teachers told us stories about village youths who had been lucky enough to get scholarships to America, to Britain and to the Soviet Union prior to Independence and immediately after Independence. Some had returned and become prominent business people or politicians in the newly liberated country, while others had never returned. Their parents waited expectedly, hoping that one day their children would return. We heard about young men and girls from poor and wealthy families who had brought glory to the village because of their education. Some people spoke bitterly about their poverty-riddled situations, which prevented their children from going to school. Each time I heard this, I felt guilty for being fortunate enough to be in school.

My father and mother worked hard on our small holding of sugarcane, sorghum and other grains, making sure to set aside enough money for our education. I continued with my secondary education, completing Form 6 with good grades in Biology, Chemistry, Physics, Maths, and English, an astonishing feat for a village girl. My aggregate points were good enough to get me into University to study microbiology as my main option. Microbiology was a novel subject for a girl to choose and I was certain that with my excellent grades, I would join University. Day after day, I waited in anticipation to get my acceptance letter, but my hopes were dashed when a letter came regretting that I had not made it to the University to do Microbiology because there was a high demand for the course and that, as a result, the cut-off points had been raised. The letter suggested I opt for Pharmacy at the medical Training Institute for which I would get a full bursary. I promptly accepted the offer. Adam's sister Sophie got a place at the University to study Literature against her parents' wish that she study medicine like her brother Adam. Sophie simply shrugged telling them she loathed the sight of blood and detested hospital smells. We both went to the city and worked hard, afraid to let down our parents and the village. Whenever we met during the weekends, Sophie talked constantly about her brother in America, showing me the latest photographs he had sent. In return, I showed her photographs of my brother Steve in India.

Ten years after he left the village, Adam returned with his medical degrees and his head filled with dreams, hopes, and visions for teaching at the School of Medicine at the University and above all to open his own private clinic. I had completed my degree in Pharmacy and was working as a Lab Assistant at the University, hoping to embark on a Masters degree. On Adam's return, Sophie introduced me to him and soon we were dating. He constantly teased me that I had blossomed from a straggly village weed into a beautiful urban rose. His Americanisms impressed me and I confided in my friends that I was head over heels in love with Adam, boasting about his promises to send me to America for postgraduate studies after our marriage. Each time I looked into my crystal-clear mirror, I saw a lovely young woman whose eyes sparkled with joy and whose smile could ignite an entire universe. I was indescribably happy. I loved listening to Adam's mellow voice explaining why he had decided to return home instead of remaining in America like many of his peers; he had returned to make a difference in our village and to provide much needed medical services to his people. But like the rest of us young people, he quickly changed his mind, saying there were no amenities, particularly electricity, in the village, each time comparing our pathetic underdeveloped village to American cites. I wondered how Adam had quickly forgotten that ten years was hardly enough time for our debt-burdened Government to have installed electricity, built tarmacked roads and shopping malls in our village.

Several months after his return from America, Adam asked my parents for my hand in marriage. Our extended family and clan members conducted negotiations for my dowry and sealed the deal with cows, goats, chickens and cash for my father, and kitchen utensils and colourful fabrics for my mother, grannies, aunties and other female beneficiaries who claimed they had participated in my upbringing. When my family calculated the dowry, I realized I was quite a costly commodity. I was the envy of the entire village and of my city friends. I walked with my head high, proud to be the expensive, prospective bride of a doctor trained in America. In the city, whenever Adam came to take me for a stroll, I swung my body provocatively, smiling wickedly at other girls' resentful, glaring faces. Their envious looks made me more audacious in my exaggerated gait. Later in my bedsit, Sophie and I would laugh hilariously at my cheekiness.

As we strolled along the city roads, I savoured the sweetness of being with Adam, relishing his expressions of undying love for me, insisting he would love me forever, no matter what troubles and tribulations we might face in the future. When we returned to the village, we went for long walks, meandering between sugarcane, bananas, sorghum and millet and vegetable plots. Out of sight of prying eyes, Adam would cup my face in his large palms and tell me how beautiful I was. When I went to the river to bathe with my friends, I admired my slim, flawless legs and arms, which shone like polished ebony. My friends told me I was a pretty girl. Back in the city, I would stare critically at myself in the mirror looking for signs of beauty. I saw a million sparkling stars in my pitch black eyes. They were full of glints when I was happy and excited and full of shadows when unhappy. Sophie sometimes warned me that I was in danger of becoming conceited and taken up with my own looks if I continued to stare constantly into my mirror. I cringed in guilt at her words, but they did not stop me imagining Adam's delight when he would finally see my gorgeous body on our wedding night.

Adam promised me a honeymoon at the coast. He wanted all his friends to know that his education in America had not been all about medicine, but about living life to its fullest. He continued to impress me with his gifts of expensive perfumes, lotions and chocolates; all of which I displayed prominently on a table in my bedsit. A couple of my friends were resentful over these gifts, spitefully questioning why Adam had chosen me to be his wife. Why not them? As they sulked and pouted, I began to ask myself the same question. Why me and not them? There was nothing special or extraordinary about me. If his choice had to do with beauty, then the village and the city were full of far more gorgeous girls than me. Why had Adam chosen me over other girls? Why hadn't he come back with an American wife? Why hadn't he chosen a girl with rich parents? Why? Why? I pushed these troublesome questions to the recesses of my mind. Sophie always supported me, urging me to ignore my spiteful friends and to never doubt Adam's love for me because she believed that he truly loved me.

Sophie was quite entwined within our lives. When Adam was still in America, he had asked her to find a suitable village girl for him since he had no desire to marry a city girl because he had heard unsavoury stories about them and he did not want to be landed with a troublesome one. Thereafter, Sophie sent him photographs of me, telling him I was the most eligible girl from our village. In turn, Sophie expected me to reciprocate by writing to my brother Steve studying in India that she was in love with him. When I hesitated, Sophie said irritably, 'listen, Eve, Adam asked me to suggest a girl from our village because he doesn't want to marry a city girl. He doesn't care if the village girl is a graduate or not, but wants one with secondary education. I looked around, and you were the most eligible girl, so that is why I sent him photos of you. Besides, since you are both in the medical field you will be as compatible as twin bananas. I want you to reciprocate by sending photos of me to your brother Steve. Tell him I am in love with him. You owe me this favour because Adam is about to marry you because I recommended you. Without my input, Adam might not be marrying you.' When it came to her own desires, Sophie never minced words. Wasting no time and not wanting to lose Adam, I sent photos and wonderful descriptions of Sophie to my brother. He was delighted with the photographs and began to correspond with her. Sophie and I giggled at our daring conspiracy. We both won.

Of course, what we did not know at the time was that my parents and Adam's had been planning our marriage for years, their only fear being that Adam might return with a wife from America. His mother's worst nightmare had been that he might return with a *white* wife. She said she wanted a daughter-in-law she could converse with, rebuke and boss about without using her son as an interpreter. She was elated when Adam returned alone. She pestered him to be honest with her and not surprise her with a white daughter-in-law lurking in the bushes waiting to be announced to the entire village. Adam told her I was the girl he planned to marry. My future mother-in-law summoned me, embraced me and gave me waist beads, informing me that the sensual touch of the beads would delight Adam on our wedding night and subsequent nights. Being a village girl, I knew the value of waist beads since both my grandmothers had frequently made them for me and taught me about me their sensual role.

Our wedding was the talk of the village. Adam decided to have two ceremonies, one in the village and one in the city. There was a reception at the village home and a reception at a leading city hotel. Adam planned the wedding to the smallest detail, leaving nothing to chance. He co-ordinated the outfits and paid for my shimmering white wedding gown, veil, shoes, and accessories. His best man and four grooms were his fellow doctors. Sophie was my maid-of-honour and my bridesmaids were her sisters, my sisters, and two nieces, all of them old enough to dance and drink the night away at the city hotel. Adam's medical colleagues and friends came in their cars to enable us have a long, impressive convoy from my home to the village church, and later to the city. One of Adam's friends drove me and Sophie to the church in a brand-new Mercedes, a gift to Adam from his parents. I felt like a princess I had read about in fairy tales.

The villagers were awestruck by the impressive wedding. They had never before seen such a grandiose wedding but agreed that since Adam's family was one of the richest families in the region, it was perfectly normal for them to hold such a wedding for their son. 'After all, when his entire clan and extended family celebrate, we also celebrate,' I heard one man proclaim. Sophie had heard people whisper that such a lavish wedding was a sheer waste of money, which could have educated needy sons and daughters of the village. As for me, people openly praised my parents for giving birth to a daughter, who had excelled in her studies, was a University graduate, and who had attracted a befitting dowry.

Truthfully, our first years of marriage were extremely happy ones. Adam worked hard at the Medical School and at a leading private hospital which paid him a good salary because of his American medical degrees. The university pay was pittance, but his position as Chief Surgeon brought him prestige. After a couple of years of hard work, he opened his own private clinic, employing two qualified doctors and a nurse to run it when he was busy elsewhere. The clinic quickly grew in popularity and he joked that it would one day develop into a hospital. And indeed, plans were drawn up and the construction is ongoing.

With Adam's busy schedule and my own work at the University Lab and occasionally helping out at our clinic, I hardly noticed imperceptible changes taking place in our life. Adam began to drink excessively and then began to verbally abuse me; constantly berating me over small issues. This soon gave way to physical abuse. On a daily basis, he lamented that I had failed to give him children. This lamentation was followed by stinging slaps. I wondered where our happiness had gone. How had it evaporated into thin air without my noticing it? How quickly had Adam forgotten our wedding vows to love me forever, in sickness and in health until death did us part? In front of his friends, he treated me lovingly, yet in the privacy of our home, he beat me brutally and hurled contemptuous words at me. I began to cringe like a frightened animal each time he entered the house. This made him so angry, inevitably he would slap me.

One Sunday morning as we ate our breakfast, he began his mocking tirade as he methodically munched his food, slowly stripping the last vestiges off two drumsticks before beginning on pieces of roasted goat meat. 'Evelyn, my sweetest wife, I should stop feeding, clothing, and housing you. After all, you have not given me any children, particularly a son. I am a total embarrassment to my friends - a total embarrassment to my extended family and clan members – a total embarrassment to my father and mother who have waited for the past ten years for their promised grandchildren - a total embarrassment to your own parents. You have failed to keep your end of the bargain. Bring my bottle of cognac.' He made his way to the living room, walking in a lumbering, uncoordinated manner because of his drunken state. At that moment, I wished he was Church-going; at least he wouldn't be drinking on a Sunday morning.

Like a lamb to the slaughter house, I followed him with the cognac and a glass.

'Evelyn, don't stand over me as if you are my Lord and Maker. Pour me a drink and sit down like a civilized being! I want to have a serious discussion with you.'

After taking a long swig of cognac, he said belligerently, 'Evelyn, you are a worthless piece of garbage. I made a huge mistake by marrying a barren woman! My parents and extended family have given up hope of ever having grandchildren from us. Mind you, Evelyn, not just any children but male heirs, preferably with my features and attributes.' He took a mouthful of cognac, swilled it in his mouth and then swallowed it slowly in a deliberate, provoking manner. He tilted back his head and deliberately burped loudly, knowing I detested this uncouth action.

I gazed at him with loathing, waiting for him to continue his discordant barrage.

'You are infertile because you had premarital sex with village boys. Do not deny it! I know village girls very well. It would take a lifetime for me to count the number of girls who enticed me to have sex with them before I left the village for America.' He took another long sip and with a snigger, continued in a garbled voice.

53

'Your barrenness is of no benefit to me. Men in my family have never failed to produce children. I know perfectly well the power of our patriarchal sperms, including my own.' He flung back his head, laughing uproariously as though he has just cracked the most hilarious joke.

I knew trouble was brewing when he looked at me with hateful bleary eyes and asked where I would be today if he hadn't rescued me from my poverty-stricken village life. 'Evelyn, my sweet wife, the only way to teach you a lesson is to give you a thorough beating as any good husband should. Don't you agree?' He downed another gulp and banged his glass on the table.

I kept quiet, as I have done for many years; my grandmothers having drummed into me the virtue of refraining from answering back or engaging in angry exchanges with my husband. If I behaved, my husband would never dream of beating me or taking a second wife. If he did beat me then that was a good sign of his love for me. With sudden clarity, I recoiled at my grandmothers' misguided load of nonsense I had failed to challenge over the years! After all, hadn't they been beaten many times? Hadn't they been cast aside like old raggedy dishcloths?

'I made a statement, dear wife, and you haven't commented. That is rude of you.'

I stood up and spoke in a low, hesitant voice. At that moment, I hated myself for my faltering voice. My vocal chords quivered as I said, 'I have undergone fertility tests and there is nothing wrong with me. Why have you have refused to undergo them?'

'My darling, darling wife, what a silly thing for you to say! Let me give you a kiss to prove my love for you.' He heaved himself from the soft leather seat, stepped close to me and gave me such a resounding slap across my face it sent me reeling against the sofa. He stepped back a few paces and stood still, a fighting bull ready to

54

charge. He yanked me to my feet and moved his face closer to mine until I felt his hot stinking breath sweep across my face. He gave me a second stinging slap. I slumped against the sofa, but quickly stood up, bracing myself for another slap, like a stunned, fettered slave unable to reply, unable to fight back. Over the years, I had become a captive unable to release myself from the tight shackles with which he had bound me. I tasted blood in my mouth and on my lips. I began to tremble uncontrollably, clenching my teeth and fists, afraid of his next blow.

'Those baby slaps should make you appreciate the fact that my parents paid good cows for you, not to mention the goats and chickens they threw in for good measure.' He flopped down and after several minutes of silence, said in a honeyed tone, 'Evelyn, my sweet wife, kindly hand me another shot of cognac.'

Quickly, I poured the cognac into his glass, spilling some on the glass table. The drops sparkled like pretty dewdrops.

Adam picked up the glass. Gently, he swilled the cognac, which sparkled iridescently. He sipped it slowly, all the while gazing intently at me. 'Listen attentively, Evelyn. I repeat - I owe you nothing - you deserve nothing because you have given me nothing.' Sloppily, he knocked back the cognac, belching in a disgusting manner. 'Are you going to disrespect me by keeping silent?' he asked, gazing at me with undisguised contempt. He burped several times.

His verbal and physical onslaught had completely frozen my senses. Tongue-tied, I stared at him, deep sadness rising within me. I asked myself if this man was truly my husband or an evil spirit come to torment me. I wished I had gone to Church; I would be free at this moment.

Adam continued, 'If I remember correctly, my parents paid your parents several high grade milking cows. Ten years is long enough for you to have produced several children. Without children, I am the laughing stock of my friends and my entire village.'

I gazed back, hating him more and more. Was he the only one who wanted children?

'The only thing that elicits any excitement from you is your cooking. You are an excellent cook. The methods you use to fry Nile perch and tilapia are unsurpassed. As for your *ugali* and greens, my goodness, I am the envy of my friends.' The words were mocking and cruel. His red eyes flickered from my head to my feet before he said languidly, 'I am no longer attracted to you, Evelyn. You need to add flesh to your bones so that I can have something soft and plump to hold onto. Rubbing against bones is not pleasant at all.' He belched loudly.

I gazed hard at this man I called my husband. His belly protruded like an obscene overgrown pumpkin. His face had become round and puffy with over-indulgence. For the first time, I realized how truly ugly he had become. An involuntary shiver ran through my body as I recalled the many nights I had acquiesced to his inept, fumbling, rough hands and his millstone body over mine. I remembered the many times I had left our conjugal bed in disgust and gone to the bathroom to shower repeatedly to rid my body of his foul perspiration of stale alcohol and the rottenness of his gluttony. Deep in my mind, I told myself that to call his fumbling exertions lovemaking would be to denigrate the exquisiteness of that word, having always believed that lovemaking should shower one with ripples of sheer pleasure and limitless waves of exuberance. I recalled that our early years of marriage had had these hallmarks. But over the years, sex with Adam had become sickeningly mundane and revolting.

As I listened to his tirade, I conversed with my innerself. *'No wonder I haven't borne any children. How can I conceive a baby with a man who has no idea about pleasuring a woman? How can I conceive a child when there is no beauty and joy in my sex life? After all, my gynaecologist told me I am not sterile.'* I have known for a long time that Adam is to blame for our childlessness – he is the infertile one, not me as proved by my fertility tests. Thoughts chased each other in my mind. Why had Adam become so cruel? Am I to blame for this? My mind raced rapidly, examining aspects of our life, trying to find reasons for the changes in Adam. Over the years, he had advanced rapidly in his chosen career and was now a renowned Professor of Surgery at the University and a visiting professor at various universities in the region. Accolades from various quarters had inflated his ego immeasurably. He had found competent doctors and nurse to run our private clinic, which was doing extremely well. Our combined earnings enabled us to live a good life, an ostentatious one. His promises of sending me to America or Britain for further studies had long ago fizzled into thin air. Instead, he sent me for driving lessons and bought me a small car, which he called my 'shopping basket' to impress our friends. He said I should be proud to work as a Pharmacist at The Memorial Hospital instead of hankering to go abroad for postgraduate studies. *'Why have things gone horribly wrong?'* I asked myself.

'Evelyn, are you listening to me?' Adam asked in a strident voice.

His words jolted me from my reverie. 'What is it now, Adam?'

'I want you to tell me why I should continue to waste good money on you. If I did not truly respect your parents, I would have sent you packing ages ago. However, they will understand why I must consider other options after ten years of marriage and still no children. I am

57

sure you already know I have a mistress.' A sneer laced his sarcastic words. There was no sign of love, no vestige of compassion for me. I saw nothing but scorn in his eyes. 'I am considering marrying my mistress so that she can give me children.'

I opened my mouth to respond, but no words formed. My throat constricted painfully. I felt truly trapped, a hapless fly caught in the unrelenting webs of a grotesque voracious spider. Surprisingly, I heard myself say in a low, controlled voice, 'you can go to hell with your mistress, Adam. I shall be kind and pray to God to give you as many children as you desire.'

Before I could say another word, he lumbered to his feet and slapped me hard, creating spinning stars around my eyes. Several slaps in quick succession snapped the taut strings around my being. From deep within me, a fire began to blaze, rousing me from my long stupor of quiescent acceptance. I distinctly heard my tensioned inner threads snap deep within me. I felt a razor-sharp knife slice through my rib cage, flooding my heart with hot blood. A red tidal wave shimmered before my eyes. I spat out the blood in my mouth, watching the red spittle stain the pristine beige carpet. Inside my head, I swore that I would kill this monster. I meant it. He had driven me to the edge of no return. I would kill him. I spat out more blood. 'Do you ever beat up your mistress?' My voice sounded alien. I watched him slump back into the leather sofa. In my mind's eye, I stamped him into an amorphous, oozing smudge. In a voice full of strength and conviction, I said, 'Adam, I have had enough of your brutality. I will never put up with it again.' The fire within me blazed harder. The ten-year cauldron of stifled emotions ruptured, leaving me emboldened, liberated, empowered. I stepped closer to Adam and said in a steel-cold voice, 'if you ever hit me again, I will kill you. I mean it.' I stared hard into his eyes and saw disbelief in them. He shrunk back. I knew he believed my words. His hands began to shake uncontrollably. I watched his mouth try to form words. He opened and shut his mouth like a fish out of water. Fear shimmered in his eyes. He reached for his glass and tremblingly poured cognac into it.

He averted his eyes. 'What nonsense are you talking, Evelyn? Get me drinking water. You know very well that if I do not drink plenty of water, I shall have a terrible hangover. Thank God it is Sunday!'

'Listen to me, Adam; if you ever hit me again, I will kill you.' My voice was colder than ice. I stared downwards into his bulging eyes and in my mind's eye, I saw a double-edged sword spin through the air and slice his head off. I saw his severed head fly through the air, hit the wall with a thud and splatter the white wall paint with an ugly red sludge. I watched the amorphous splatter, bit by bit transform itself into an ugly grotesque monster bearing Adam's rotund body and features. I continued to stare at him with revulsion. With greater conviction, I said, 'I refuse to take any more of your brutality. It ends *now*. When I say I will kill you if you ever hit me again, I mean every single word. I will be quite happy to spend the rest of my life in jail.'

Silently, he gazed back at me, distinct apprehension in his eyes. After a while, he laughed derisively. 'Sweetie, be a darling and make me a cup of coffee while I think over what you have just told me. After that, you can repeat what you have just told me, my darling wife. My beautiful Evelyn, stop staring at me with those cruel snake eyes and get me coffee. My head is spinning from too much cognac.' He picked up a medical journal and casually flipped the pages, like a contrite child playing with a toy after a severe scolding. His hands were shaking. Soon, the trembling spread through his entire body. He put down the journal, leaned back on the sofa and closed his eyes. 'Evelyn dearest, get me a jug of water. My head is pounding.'

'Adam, you know the direction of the kitchen. And you need not remind me that the kitchen with all its utensils, gadgets, etcetera, etcetera, is all yours. I am going to shower.' I could not believe that this was Evelyn speaking. Evelyn had actually stood up to Adam. Then I realized that it was Eve talking; that Eve had emerged from Evelyn's shadow. Unlike Evelyn, Eve had the guts and gall to confront her husband. Eve had freed Evelyn from Adam's stranglehold. Evelyn flew out of the open window leaving Eve behind to face the raging bull.

As I turned to leave, Adam leapt to his feet, all trace of drunkenness gone. He lurched at me. I stepped back, tripping over the coffee table. I lay on my back on the carpet watching him advance towards me. The next thing, he was raining kicks at my upturned face. All the courage I had mustered evaporated. My bravado rapidly dissipated. I was back at ground zero, trapped, unable to free myself. I shrank back like a wounded, defenceless animal, covered my face with my hands to shield myself from his vicious kicks, and curled myself into a tight ball. Kick after kick. Kick after kick. Kick after kick. Kick after kick. His crude expletives hurt me as much as each brutal kick. I stifled my groans, determined to endure it all; determined to show him I was not afraid of him. After one last ruthless kick, he called me a slut and left the living room. I heard the car start and drive away. No doubt he had left to visit his mistress.

I tried to sit up, but my chest felt as if it had caved in. Shafts of pain tore through my back. I suppressed my screams of pain. I took a few breaths, struggled again to sit up, but the pain was excruciating. I lay still for agonizing minutes. Try as hard as I could, I was unable to sit up. Finally, inch by inch, I crawled to the nearby guests' bathroom. Once inside, I forced myself to stand up. Gingerly, I sat on the edge of the bathtub. Once strength flowed into my body, I straightened up, and splashed my face with cold water. I breathed in and out until the pain subsided. I took a hard look at myself in the mirror. The eyes staring back were dead. There were no sparkling glints in them. They were cold, grey, and lifeless. My face was swollen, my nose bloody. Blood had had trickled down the corners of my mouth and drip-dropped onto my white blouse. I leaned closer to the mirror, gazing at my twin-self staring back. My twin-self was frozen, lifeless, with despair and desperation in her eyes. I watched tears cruise down her face. Feeling terribly sad for her, I reached towards the mirror, and tried to erase her tears, but could not.

I heard my twin-self ask me questions, 'Eve, what went wrong? Did that monster really love you when he married you? Have you ever truly loved that brute? Why didn't you leave him when he began to brutalize you? Why have you accepted his contemptuous tirades and cruelty for an eternity?' I remained mute, my chest heaving painfully, my eyes dry and gritty. There were bloody tears on her cheeks and at the corners of her mouth and eyes. 'God, don't let her go blind,' I pleaded.

I turned away from my anguished twin-self and splashed cold water on my face. My knees buckled under me and I sank to the bathroom floor, memories flooding my mind, taking me back to those golden days of blissful courting; back to happy days when Adam constantly whispered sweet nothings into my eager, attentive ears. I recalled the days when we were in love; my parents' joyful faces when Adam, with a bag of medical degrees from America, asked them if he could marry me. I recalled how they held their heads high, each time boasting to friends and neighbours that Adam had come straight from the airport to our home to ask for my hand in marriage. They created and recreated stories, adding plenty of spice to them. They told all and sundry that Adam had proclaimed I was the most stunning girl in the village. With beaming pride, they said Adam wanted me because I was a University graduate. 'How many girls in our village are graduates?' my mother would ask anyone willing to listen to her.

I remembered that I too swam in the brilliant sunshine that lit the dullest spots of our lives and turned them into shimmering golden pools of future opportunities and blessings. I too held my head high, surreptitiously glancing at my friends' envious faces; secretly waiting for them to express their jealousy. I became a show-off, strutting around the village, arrogantly boasting that Adam had really wanted to live in America but had come back because of me. Now, as the coldness of the ceramic bathroom tiles soothed my body, I scolded myself for such arrogance, but just as quickly, told myself it was in the psyche of Lakeside people to be arrogant.

I stared at my puffy face in the mirror, recalling how Adam, fresh-faced twenty-three year old youth full of smiles and dreams, had left for America and returned a surgeon oozing with smugness and a pronounced American twang. Above all, his achievements helped to assuage his father's constant lament that he himself had missed the opportunity to go to America via the American-sponsored airlifts in the early 1960s; claiming that malicious upcoming politicians had denied him the chance. While others of his friends had gone via airlifts to the Soviet Union, he had had remained in the village despite having performed well in the Colonial Junior Primary Certificate exams. For years, he vented his frustrations at all and sundry. 'Tell me if I wasn't the cleverest young man in the whole of this village.' People agreed that Adam's father been extraordinarily clever and should have had a chance for further education abroad. Fortunately, he had been astute enough to make good use of the land inherited from his father and had become wealthy through agriculture and rich enough to send Adam to America, proud that he had no need to beg the Government for a scholarship for his son, feeling justified to revel in Adam's success, constantly reminding the entire village about his brilliant American-trained son.

My mind kept repeating things. It told me that at the beginning of our marriage, my husband constantly brought me gifts and took me to expensive restaurants for meals. During Valentine's Day, he brought me bunches of roses, telling me stories about wonderful Valentine Days he had experienced in America. I waited for the most precious gift he had promised me - the gift of postgraduate studies abroad. I begged, I cajoled, reminding him about his promise to me and to my parents. He never went beyond the promise of 'yes, Evelyn, you will go to university soon in America or Europe. There is plenty of time. Enjoy life, Evelyn; do not stress yourself over postgraduate studies. Look at what you have - a beautiful home, cars and a driver to take you wherever you want to go. And you have a BSc degree. What more do your really require? Isn't my love enough, my sweet wife?' Year after year, I begged, but nothing happened. Eventually, I stopped asking him about my postgraduate studies and he never mentioned the matter again. Gradually, like a snail making its way across a gritty path, the gifts, the roses, and the dinners in expensive restaurants all dwindled. The pleasurable things in my life ended with a thud.

Just as gradually, my husband underwent a transformation, metamorphosing into a sullen stranger; arriving home later and later each night, until a time came when he sometimes never came home at all. He always had a reason for his absences, pointing out his busy schedule as a surgeon as the main culprit. I never sought the veracity of his excuses or his hospital schedule. At first, I smilingly accepted them, but then started to get irritated and then angry. After some time, I actually looked forward to them because they gave me the freedom to dream my dreams; freedom to be myself; freedom to rest my wounded self; freedom to reclaim myself for myself.

One of the changes in Adam was that he began to complain that he had made a mistake to return to Africa from America. Had he stayed in America, he would have become extremely wealthy; there he would be a highly respected surgeon; he would not be facing daily hassles of incompetence and lack of amenities in this 'blasted, backward country of *yours*!' Time and time again, he forgot that he had told me all about the difficulties he had faced in America, especially as a foreign black doctor who found it next to impossible to advance in the medical world. He forgot he had told me about the pervasive racist attitudes in South Carolina where he had studied medicine. He forgot why he had decided to come home - to help foster the growth of medicine and science. He forgot his dreams and vision of contributing to the advances being made in medicine throughout Africa. He talked as if he was not born of this country, as if he was not a son of the African soil, as if he were a foreigner in his own land.

Adam's constant yearnings for America irritated me to the point of wanting to slap sense into his head. He was always lamenting, 'I am going back to America.' Not once did he ever say 'we will go to America.' It was always 'I will return to America'. I was not included in his plans to return to America. I was simply a sounding board for his outbursts; a patient, listening idiot for his dissatisfaction and frustration with our country, which, at first, I understood and sympathized with, but which finally dulled my senses with their frequency and irrationality. To combat his frustrations, Adam organized frequent ostentatious meat-roasting feasts at our home; our many friends coming to consume beer, alcohol, sodas, and the choicest cuts of beef, goat meat, chicken and fish served with salads, greens, rice, chapatis, and ugali. I too enjoyed the parties as much as our friends did since the parties relieved my growing loneliness and constant gnawing distress at my unfulfilled dreams to embark on a Masters and then a PhD in Microbiology.

Now, lying flat on my back on the cold ceramic tiled bathroom floor, I evoke my long ago dream of making something of myself. I had extinguished my dream of going abroad for further studies. Silently, I rebuke myself for not making Adam keep his promise, berating myself for never having had the courage to insist on undertaking further studies.

Disgusted at my own lack of self-motivation, I get off the cold floor and gently wash the blood off my face, wincing at the painful, puffy bruises. I splash warm water on my face. I cannot hold back my scalding tears. I move closer to the mirror and take a hard, long look at my bruised face. I feel a deep, gaping hole open up inside me. It is a bottomless vacuum bereft of feelings. I weep, making choking, rasping sounds.

Seemingly out of the blue, rage erupts within me, leaps to life, fires me up, and sets me ablaze. It is a rage I have never experienced before. It is a rage that I know will cost Adam his life if he dares to come anywhere near me, if he dares to touch me. I sit on the edge of the bathtub and take deep breaths until my rage subsides. I run a hot bath, pour dollops of pine-scented bath foam into the water, and stir it slowly, thoughtfully, and mechanically. Painfully, I slip off my clothes, step into the tub, recline full-length and let the hot, pine-scented frothy water seep into my battered body. I grit my teeth at the sudden burning pain as the water comes in contact with my bruises. After a while, the pain disappears. I close my eyes and began to work out a strategy for leaving Adam, for freeing myself from the fetters with which he has shackled me. Piece by piece, I build up a mosaic of my game plan to break free from my imprisonment, claim back my life and fulfil my long-cherished dreams. Piece by piece, the strategy coalesces into a recognizable form; each piece strategically slotting into its own unique place. I itemize things in my mind. Escape from my dungeon of despair. A place of my own. Best woman lawyer in town. Bank accounts. Visa and university application forms. I sigh thoughtfully, wondering about the feasibility of it all. I take a deep, deep breath, hold it until my lungs are ready to explode, and exhale. Searing pain from my bruised chest shoots to the crown of my head. I clench my teeth. The pain decides my future, irrevocably. There is no turning back.

I get out of the bath, go to my bedroom, and dress in a white cotton skirt and white silk blouse, and make my way to my beloved jacaranda trees. Masses of blossoms have carpeted the grass beneath the trees. I lie flat on my sore back on the squishy carpet of blossoms and slowly wriggle my body into its luxurious softness. The softness of the carpet of blossoms soothes my sore, bruised back. I take a handful of jacaranda blossoms and gently rub my face with them. They ease my bruises. Gazing upwards at the scintillating mass of jacaranda blossoms, I remember an Amazonian myth about Mitu, a beautiful bird who landed on a jacaranda tree, bringing with him a lovely woman, the priestess of the moon. The priestess descended from the tree to live among the Amazonian villagers, imparting knowledge and teaching them ethics. Having fulfilled her mission, she returned to the tree adorned in jacaranda blooms and ascended to the heavens to unite with her soulmate, the son of the sun. I guess they lived happily ever after.

Suddenly, I want to be that priestess adorned in jacaranda blossoms. I shade my eyes with my hand, looking upwards, hoping to see the priestess, hoping to gain valuable insights from her. Through the sun-dappled blossoms, I see her waving to me. But sadness overwhelms me at the thought of her imminent departure. I whisper to her to stay but she quickly disappears into the mass of brilliant mauve-blue blossoms. I blink my eyes to bring me to the present.

I remove my white blouse and examine the lovely purplish blue stain. The stain has created a lovely picture of a purplish butterfly. I hang the blouse on a nearby branch and lie flat on my back, on the carpet of soft blossoms. Taking deep breaths, I close my eyes. At this precise moment, I see myself erupting out of Adam's dungeon and fly away, soaring far beyond the clouds, far beyond his outstretched, lethal arms.

The blueness of the jacarandas and my Eve-ness assuages my anguished, raw soul. Far up in the cerulean sky, I flap my phoenix wings in exhilaration; celebrating my name; pronouncing it ever so gently, ever so softly. I celebrate the goodness of my essence. I celebrate the goodness of being woman. I hear the jacaranda blossoms gently, unhurriedly, rhythmically fall to the ground, electrifying the grass into a startling contrast of purples and luminous green. The jacarandas whisper that their blue symphony can only be heard by someone in deepest pain. Softly, they urge me to come back from my safe haven in the sky and lie under their welcoming shade. I soar downwards, feeling the breeze of freedom beneath my outstretched arms.

Once under the tree, I lie on my back and push away all sad thoughts out of my mind. As I shut my eyes, I hear the soft symphony of the jacarandas. It is as if I am in a cathedral with amazing acoustics. Ever so quietly I sing my song of freedom, whispering over and over and over again, 'I am Eve. I am Eve. *I am Eve.*' Before long, my whisper becomes a reverberating song of liberation. I feel velvety jacaranda blossoms fall on my tear-streaked face. Soon, I am swathed in a magnificent robe of mauve-blue blossoms, as light as a gentle breeze, as weightless as gossamer silk, as buoyant as my spirit flying through the air.

CHAPTER FOUR

Sarah

Until this morning, I was still battling to fully comprehend what happened to me in early March two years ago during the season of the jacarandas, when the trees dazzled me with their surreal beauty, driving me into an obsessive love affair; a love affair which etched my soul with unbelievable joy and searing anguish. For the past two years, I have tried to dig for answers buried deep within my soul, in order to assuage my agony.

Immediately after the affair ended, I told myself it was imperative to write all about it, to explain to my logical self why the jacarandas drove me into a frenzied love affair; a fanatical love I clung to with all my might. In that season, I distinctly heard the jacarandas urge me to unfurl my shrivelled wings and fly to the moon, fly to the stars, far, far away from my humdrum, boring, unfilled life; my life devoid of love, joy, and excitement. They prompted me to become a phoenix and soar high.

When I gazed at their mauve-blue blossoms with focused eyes, I saw them waving to me, heard them whispering secrets into my attentive ears, telling me life is brief, life is unsure, life is a tormentor which must be challenged and defeated; life must be enjoyed to its fullest. I strained my ears harder to hear their words.

I heard them urge me to capture fleeting happiness, no matter how transient, no matter how painful to attain. In that March season, the jacaranda trees invited me into their interlacing labyrinth of wonderment and uncertainty, tightly holding me captive within their arms, unwilling to let me escape. They wove an awesome, glistening mauve-blue web around me, tossing me a kaleidoscopic invitation to follow them into Aphrodite's alluring garden in Cythera ablaze with a million iridescent mauve-blue blossoms beckoning me to dance a capricious love dance with them. Following eagerly and blindly, I soon fell into their bewitching snare. I danced madly; danced frenziedly like a possessed demon, my eyes fixed on the stunningly beautiful Aphrodite adorned in mauve-blue blossoms.

She welcomed me into her garden, imploring me to dance with her. After the intoxicating dance, she festooned me with a thousand purple blossoms, promising me that my Ares would soon be at my side. Sighing rapturously, and with renewed hope flooding my being, I fell into an all-embracing, drunken stupor. That was the beginning of my madness; the beginning of my obsession; the beginning of my anguish.

After the affair, I promised myself I would immediately capture my madness on paper, on canvas, on video, on anything tangible. I would express how the jacarandas made me drunk with love, with joy, and with inexplicable throbbing pain. I would illustrate in minute detail the bell-shaped blossoms; describe in painstaking detail their dazzling mauve-blueness; explain how they carpeted my way to obsessive happiness, to euphoria I had never before experienced. I would capture the beauty and the ugliness of the illicit affair. I would evoke the dizzying scent of bouquets of roses and the lingering fragrance of a single unblemished rose left on my gate to tell me he had been and 'bounced'. I pledged to remember his quirky smile, his warm chuckle, his teasing banter –especially when I pointed out the breathtaking beauty of the jacarandas. He would cup my face with his warm hands and say, 'do you know you are crazy? Why should I take notice of jacarandas when they are an integral part of my African life? And I am a man at that! African men have no time for admiring flowers!' And then, very gently, he would tilt my head with his hands and ask tenderly, 'will you love me intensely if I bring you masses of jacaranda blossoms? Will you?'

One time, wanting to shock him, I said, 'when I die, I want you to cover my body and my grave with bunches of jacaranda blossoms.' Before I could continue, he clapped his hand tightly over my mouth, imploring me never to talk about death in his presence. I nodded, but vividly pictured my body and grave covered in lovely jacaranda blossoms. I sighed in anticipation.

More than two years have gone by and I have not yet found answers to soothe my inner turmoil. In vain, I have tried to capture, in distilled images and expressive words, my joy and my emptiness. I still do not comprehend what happened to me during that season of the jacarandas when they dazzled me with their surreal beauty, driving me into the obsessive love affair. I told myself it was imperative to write all about it; to explain to my logical self why the jacarandas drove me into a frenzied affair; a fanatical love I clung to with all my might, refusing to believe it had ended irretrievably. In that season, I kept hearing the jacarandas distinctly exhort me to unfurl my shrivelled wings and fly far, far away from my humdrum, boring, unfilled life; fly to place where exhilarating joy was waiting for me. One day, standing under the jacarandas, I unfurled my wings and flew away, finally landing in a foreign country full of tantalizing promises of happiness. Was it a dream?

Yesterday, I gazed long and hard at the jacarandas which burst into bloom early in the week. Some, I suspect, are waiting for the others to display their glory before they themselves burst into even more spectacular wonder. As I gazed at their brilliant mauve-blue blossoms, they seemed to prod my mind, begging me to collect the scattered fragments of my memories and fit them into a glorious mosaic to replace the lacklustre one etched deep in my heart. My continued anguish became heightened by their dazzling mauve-blues and later in the evening, a scattering of dark purplish blossoms on my pristine green lawn mirrored my sorrow; a deep gnawing, throbbing pain.

With which words or images could I possibly describe the excruciating pain carved deep within my soul? What part did the mauve-blue blossoms play in the affair? If indeed they played a part, could I betray their fleeting exquisiteness by inscribing my own pain upon them? Each time I asked this question, my scalding tears of pain told me I could not. Why do I feel the need to coalesce my memories into something meaningful with shafts of sheer joy and barbs of cutting despair? Why do I want to recreate a love that became an enslaving demon? This morning, I forced myself to think of possible reasons. Perhaps, I need to evoke the memories to ease my anguish. Possibly, I want to transform them into significant mementoes, embellishing them with a tinge of gold to render them valuable commodities, priceless artefacts to ensconce forever deep within my soul. Maybe, just maybe, I need to find a tiny space of refuge in the Garden of Cythera to contain my unspeakable pain which often bubbles up when I recall the utter bliss of the affair.

A period of two years has not been enough time to rid myself of him. As a myriad questions raced through my tortured mind, my pain returned, stabbing me mercilessly. I rushed outside to seek refuge and solace under the embracing shade of the jacarandas. I lay face-down on the fallen blossoms and wept bitterly.

Later, in the quietness of my garden, a reason slowly began to form within me, a fragment to add to the slowly-emerging mosaic. Fragments began to come together, began to take definite shape. My heart whispered that I would soon find answers. As I sipped my coffee, the beauty of the jacarandas almost suffocated me. The mass of mauve-blue blossoms made me catch my breath, convinced they were reminding me that I had not kept the promise I made to myself after the break-up.

I looked away from the questioning jacarandas, not wanting to remember anything; but my mind forced me to recall that it was just before the onset of the March rains that I plummeted into the affair. I recalled watching the fernlike leaves of the trees turn a luminous green before they dropped off, leaving the bare trees looking like skeletal sculptures implanted into the landscape. I recollected how the first whisper of blossoms was a clear sign that the rains were about to begin. Sure enough, soon after, the naked trees burst into a breathtaking indefinable mass of ever-changing mauve-blues against the brilliant blueness of the African sky. Later in the week, when the first drizzles of rain fell gently, the bell-shaped blossoms also fell, softly carpeting my lawn. Yesterday, when I drove along the city avenues, I gasped at the beauty of the trees and the carpet of blue blossoms on the tarmac. The sight left me intoxicated, breathless and lightheaded.

I drained my coffee, marvelling that in bright sunlight, the jacaranda blossoms are surreal, ethereal, and magical. The sight always leaves me gasping, making me want to live forever; making me wish I were a musician with the ability to create a glorious symphony in cadences of blues and mauves. When I gaze at the blossoms, it is as if this is the first and last time I will ever behold such exquisiteness. Invariably, tears of joy and excruciating pain cruise down my cheeks. Sometimes, I rush to the mirror to check if my tears are the colour of the jacaranda blossoms and, sometimes, they shockingly are mauve-blue.

After making another cup of coffee, I recalled that after a bad drought and oppressively hot days, the jacaran-

73

das are even more spectacular. Each sip of my coffee jolted my senses and assailed my mind with crystal-clear memories. In that season of the affair, the jacarandas were splendid beyond belief. They continued to bloom well into the last week of April, scattering their blossoms on sidewalks, avenues, and lawns. The Nairobi environs had never looked lovelier. I especially loved driving down the Muthaiga valley and looking up at slopes filled with flowering jacaranda trees. In that season, I silently thanked the colonialists for their foresight in planting jacarandas along the city avenues; I silently thanked property developers for planting them in gardens and parks. Sadly now, our City Fathers have cut down most of the trees to make way for skyscrapers and super highways as if concrete and tarmac are more beautiful and enriching than beautiful trees and shrubs.

Now, I am determined to write down what I promised myself back then. I will start with my name. I breathe deeply and say, 'my name is Sarah.' I doubt that there is anything Biblical about its choice, but I do smile at its Hebrew meaning of 'Princess' or 'noblewoman' because, with my rather chaotic lifestyle and lack of manicures and pedicures, I am a far cry from being a princess; but I do like the Sanskrit meaning of 'essence' or 'core'. My mother, a regular churchgoer, always claims she named me for the Sarah in the Bible. Once, when I was a young girl and complained that I did not like the name because it sounded so commonplace, she implored me to read the Bible and discover its true meaning. When I grew older, I read that God changed the name from Sarai to Sarah as part of a covenant after Hagar bore Abraham his first son Ishmael. I wondered if my mother had wanted to imply that she hoped I would become a noblewoman instead of a harum-scarum.

My mind will not allow me to write down my memories. Instead, it evokes the words of my ultra Afrocentric African-American friends, who fled from America to settle permanently in my country. They disparage my name as nothing but a colonial one, which I should have discarded a long time ago. One of them, Maarifa, berates me each time he meets me, impressing upon me that he *and* his wife *and* children all bear *real* African names, boasting, rather pompously, that through their African names, he can pinpoint their precise ancestral home and heritage located somewhere in Ukambani. He tells me that my mindset is too colonial because I refuse to rid myself of the Christian name. 'Why, why, don't you use you African name Pendo?' he never fails to ask belligerently. He talks as if my Christian name denies me my heritage. I usually tease him that that he simply lifted words from a dictionary and turned them into names, asking him what is in a name after all. After all, a rose by any other name is a rose, is a rose, is a rose, *is* a rose, isn't it?

I never fail to remind Maarifa that even though many of our names do pinpoint our different ethnic groups, our country is a melting pot of sorts: you never can tell from where precisely people originated; even the most ardent indigenes cannot accurately pinpoint their origins. Maarifa always snorts in disgust at my dismissive attitude, telling me I need to decolonize my mind; a challenge that makes me roar in laughter. But he continues challenging me, forcing me to consider my flippant stand, forcing me to reflect, making me concede that there is some truth in his words.

Nodding slowly, I agree that British colonialism destabilized us, colonized our minds, altered our psyche, and turned our heads 360 degrees. We are still rotating, spinning here and there, unsure who we truly are. Independence came and the black nouveau-riches stepped into the shoes of the colonizers, some quickly growing into rotund Fat Cats on 10 percent deals and stolen national wealth. Foreign investors, ex-colonizers and their children and grandchildren continue to enjoy the best parts of our country, the sunshine, the beaches, the wildlife, and above all, without mincing words, as Maarifa would say, their subservient servants. He points out that they set themselves apart from the rest of society through their ultra-European-ness and their ultra-expatriate attitudes and they live in exclusive, serene leafy suburbs and in wild life conservancies with vast acreage.

Maarifa never fails to remind me that these *wazungu* behave as if they are still living in the Happy Valley era and that although we are an independent nation, it is as if colonialism never died. I have to agree with him on that particular point.

In the sprawling slums, scattered throughout the republic, the ordinary people continue to languish in poverty, wondering how the hard-won fruits of independence slipped through their outstretched palms and how it is that foreigners continue to own thousands of acres. Despite Maarifa's irritating self-righteous ways, he constantly ignites my mind with his probing questions. When his wife Malaika joins us, her animated voice and balanced opinions mesmerize me, leaving me feeling I am a total ignoramus and mentally-colonized.

'Sarah' I say aloud, 'will you stop rambling on in your mind and start writing down your memories?' I gaze out of my window at my splendid jacaranda trees covered in their mass of mauve-blue blossoms. The sight reminds of last week when I passed through our fourth largest town on my way to my *oshago*, to my upcountry home. The jacarandas lining the highway were spectacular. Sadly, in the next little township, with a multitude of little businesses in the form of open-air bicycle repair marts, assorted kiosks, vegetable and fruit kiosks and woebegone-looking *dukas* with rusty iron sheets adorning the roofs, the jacarandas looked bedraggled and sparse; their hacked off large branches showing evidence that charcoal-makers and firewood sellers, hell-bent on making their riches from the remaining trees, had been busy. Yet, guiltily I remembered that I too frequently stop to buy a sack of charcoal, never questioning from which unfortunate trees it came. My blatant contradictions prick my conscience. I tell myself Maarifa would chortle in satisfaction.

'Sarah, get back to writing!' I close my eyes tightly and breathe deeply. Very slowly, tiny scraps of scattered thoughts begin to coalesce. Before long, I realize that deep within my soul, I know the reasons why I want to capture those fleeting memories; I need to dull the pain and the wretchedness of the affair; I need to stem the bleeding wound in my innermost soul; but all along, I was too afraid to commit myself to paper, to film, to video, to canvas; too reluctant to unravel my pain and feelings of acute guilt. My fears stopped me from unravelling myself, exposing myself to myself, staring face-to-face with myself. It was best to keep my bittersweet memories in the very recesses of my mind; far healthier to forget the entire affair. But could I?

I would be lying if I said it is possible to forget an affair. I will never truly forget it. I continue to weep tears of desperation because I still love him; I constantly craving to have him by my side. My love for him stretches beyond the boundaries of my heart. When silence surrounds me in the dark hours of the night, I reach out for him, hoping against hope that he has sneaked into my bed. When my hands touch nothingness, I weep uncontrollably. How stupid am I?

I look at the blossom-laden jacarandas outside my window and tell myself I will gaze into the depths of my mirror and confront the memories of the affair. I will endeavour to understand my obsession with him. I will examine why I allowed him to take me to the mountain-top of ecstasy knowing full-well he could never truly be mine. Why did I curl into a cocoon of desolation after he went back to his comfort zone, back to his wife wearing his wedding ring?

I ask aloud, 'what is it about us women? Why do we do this to ourselves? Why do we give and give and give and after giving and losing, we evoke the pain over and over again? Why do we keep nothing ourselves? Why do we seek nothing for ourselves?' Painful silence greets me.

How did the affair start? Why did it start? When did it start? How did it end? Why did it end? I stare out of my window at the jacarandas, looking for answers. Their mauve-purple blossoms galvanize me to alertness. Tangible, transitory memories, like shimmering mirages, flood my mind. They fall from my mind into my hands. I hold them tenderly, beautiful little mementoes; tiny, sparkling precious gems glittering with love and pain engraved on them; little gems all too soon gone. My heart races and I am back in the arms of my lover, savouring every embrace, every kiss, every whisper of love. The memories erase the excruciating pain that assailed me minutes before. My heart flutters, beats, pounds. The two years of the affair inexplicably coalesce into today, into now. Two years of ecstasy and intermittent pain-filled liaisons collapse into this very second. My eyes blur with tears.

I remember moments of sheer fulfilment and moments of downright desolation. I blink and refocus my eyes, staring hard at the jacarandas. Their beauty lacerates me, creating agony deep within my soul. My invisible ex-lover quickly invades my being, taking up every available space within my mind, within my soul, within my throbbing heart. He is a spectre clinging tightly, tightly to me, suffocating my soul. I am unable to chase him away; he is too embedded within my being. I close my eyes to shut him out, but he is there, smiling sweetly at me, kissing me tenderly, regaling me with humorous jokes, tickling me all over me until I scream out for him to stop, reminding him how much I hate being tickled in my ribs. He is a dancing demon in my mind. I implore him to leave me alone, but he refuses to.

Memories quickly take me back to that season. I was at my most vulnerable when the affair started. It was a bad period in my life. I was in-between-jobs, as the Americans love to say. My life was a series of ups and downs. I went to see him on the recommendation of a friend, after I told her I needed to see a good general practitioner because my own doctor was on leave; that I was feeling wretched, utterly unwell. She recommended her own GP. Immediately she mentioned the doctor's names, I cried out aloud in disbelief, opening my eyes saucer-wide.

'I know him!' I exclaimed. 'We used to be good friends, but it is about eighteen years since I last saw him. Gosh, how weird! I can't believe it.' And truly, I could not believe it.

'That is why you should go and see him. He is an excellent doctor and one of the very few I really trust,' continued my friend, giving me a wide conspiratorial smile as she said, 'and he is quite cute!' She searched through her cellphone, scribbled down the numbers and told me his offices were at Millennium Plaza, a popular ultra-shopping complex in an upmarket suburb; a shopping complex I frequented for coffee and snacks with friends. How odd that I had never run across him!

When I got home, I debated if I should call him. I had actually forgotten him. Did I really want to go and see him after all these years? Pushing aside my uncertainty, I took a few deep breaths and called one of his numbers. A receptionist answered and I asked for the doctor. She put me through. 'Is this Doctor Richard?' I asked in trepidation.

'Can I help you?' I recognized his voice immediately. Rising warmth suffused my body. My mind began to relive the past at an incredible speed...far, far back in my mind, I saw his teasing smile. I am back in London, in a students' university hall where we lived when doing our doctoral studies. A series of images flood my mind – in the evening, after a hard day of lectures, we are in a pub across the road playing scrabble - we are in Finsbury Park taking photographs besides the summer roses - we are sitting on a bench in Queensbury Park enjoying the summer sun and eating strawberries - we are in my room or in his room, talking, laughing, and cracking jokes. Memories of our closeness swarm my mind. I hear the voice of one of my closest friends telling me I am spending too much time with Richard; there is a distinct tinge of jealousy in his voice, in his attitude, in the way he looks at me as though I am betraying him. He is right because since Richard and I became close, I hardly spend time with my other friends. My time is consumed by Richard. Each time, I make lame excuses.

'Hallo? Are you still there? Richard's voice brought me abruptly to the present moment.

'Yes, I am. My name is Sarah. I am not sure if you remember me. We lived in the same students' hall in London years ago.' The words tumbled out of my mouth and I talked fast in order not to be tempted to switch off my phone. I was sure he could hear my heart pounding.

'Of course I remember you, why wouldn't I? It has been many years since I last saw you.'

'Yes, it is a long time ago,' I replied. I heard no hint of surprise in his low voice. Instead, his warm smile flashed across the distance that separated us, making my heart throb harder. 'I would like to make an appointment to come and see you. My doctor is on leave.' There was a slight quiver in my voice and my hand holding the phone began to feel clammy.

'When and what time?' he asked, sounding professionally detached.

I told him the next morning would suit me. I heard him ask someone about fitting me in. A few minutes later, he told me 9.30 a.m. was all right. I thanked him and hung up. Suddenly, I realized I was afraid of meeting him again. As I searched myself, I knew I was afraid of the memory of a short-lived fling we had had in London. My heart started pounding harder at the recollection of this short-lived fling. Had he thought about me over the years? Did he remember anything at all?

Next morning, I woke up early, had a bath, and dressed with care; becoming agitated when it occurred to me that Richard would have to examine me. Because of this, I chose my clothing carefully, deciding on white lacy lingerie, a white skirt, a white top, and a red jacket to break the monotony of the white. I sprayed my favourite perfume behind my ears. The delicate fragrance perked me up, giving me confidence. Surely, I was brave enough to confront a whole army, including Richard, wasn't I? I leaned closer to my mirror, gazing long at myself. Furrows of worry lined my face.

Before I left the house, I glanced out of the window to make sure it wasn't going to rain. The month of March can be notorious for sudden showers or heavy deluges. Fortunately, the sky was a clear blue, promising to be a sunny day. From a child, my parents had taught me that when the African sky is a certain blistering blue, it is a sure indication that the sun will shine brightly. I whispered to the jacaranda blossoms not to herald the rain yet. I needed plenty of sunshine to bolster my flagging spirits. The drive to Millennium Plaza is usually uneventful but can be hell if there is a traffic jam along the highway. On that particular morning, I was glad the inevitable traffic jam had petered out. I parked in the basement of the Plaza and took the lift to the third floor, occupied by the medical fraternity.

There were golden plaques engraved with the names of gynaecologists, paediatricians, skin specialists, dentists, and ophthalmologists. I located Richard's name and headed in the direction of the arrow indicating the South Wing. I walked along a well-lit corridor until I saw his name engraved on a plaque on a door. I knocked, pushed open the door and entered the spacious reception area with its black leather chairs. A young receptionist welcomed me with a warm smile and greetings. Nervously, I introduced myself. She handed me a medical card requiring personal details and a brief medical history. I carefully filled out the form and handed it back. She disappeared into the doctor's office and soon returned to usher me into the doctor's office. And there was Richard reading a newspaper. He looked up, smiling broadly at me. Butterflies fluttered in my stomach as I gazed back, observing that he had hardly changed since the last time I saw him in London. I sat down, wondering if he would notice any major changes in me.

'How have you been all these years?' There was no hint of excitement in his voice despite the smile on his face. He played with his fountain pen. Apparently, he had been doing the crossword puzzle. I recalled that even in London, he never failed to do the crossword puzzles.

'Fine, fine, but right now, I have a bad chest infection.' I felt shy and awkward, as if talking to a stranger. In fact, it would have been much easier to talk to a total stranger. 'How have you been?'

'I am great. No complaints.' He titled his head slightly to scrutinize me. 'A while back, I read an article in a newspaper that you have become a famous environmentalist. Where do you work?'

'At an environmental NGO working on safeguarding our water catchment areas; in other words, working towards reclaiming our indigenous forests.' I stared at photographs lining a wall. There were several of him, a woman and children. I looked at him and asked, 'are you still lecturing at the University, or is your clinic too lucrative to bother with teaching?'

'I devote two days a week to lectures. My clinic keeps me very busy. Anyway, I suppose I had better examine you.' He suddenly sounded nervous. He looked at his watch. 'You said you have a bad chest infection. How long have you had it?'

'Almost two weeks now.' I explained that I was feeling generally run down. After jotting down notes, he called the nurse to show me to the examination room, instructing her to first take my blood pressure. She helped me to remove my jacket, propped up the pillow, covered me with a white sheet, and took my blood pressure, which she wrote down on a medical pad. When the doctor entered, she stepped away from the examination bed, keeping discreetly in the background. Nowadays, medical ethics require nurses to be in the consultation room. I was glad for her presence.

Richard slipped on surgical gloves. 'Nurse, pull up her blouse. The stethoscope is cold so it will probably make you jump,' he warned as he began to examine me after the nurse had rolled up my blouse to my chin.

'Does your chest hurt when you breathe?' he asked.

I nodded, feeling uncomfortable as his eyes stared into mine. He told me to sit up and to take a deep breath and hold it. He prodded me here and there instructing me when to breathe. This was routine procedure, yet embarrassment flooded my entire body. I wondered if he was looking at my breasts and if so, what his thoughts were. I felt ashamed at my own introspections. Being at a vantage point, I could look up closely at him. I saw beads of sweat on his brow, a sign that he too was feeling awkward. His touch was gentle as he examined me.

He completed the examination, told me to get dressed, and to follow him to his office. He walked out of the room, pulling off the surgical gloves and dropping them into a medical waste bin. The nurse helped me put on my jacket and I joined Richard in his office, sitting down gingerly in acute discomfort.

'From my examination, there is nothing seriously wrong with you but you do have a very congested chest. Your blood pressure is slightly elevated, but nothing to worry about. I will prescribe antibiotics for ten days to clear your chest. Additionally, I am prescribing Vitamin B complex and Vitamin C to supplement fresh fruit and vegetables. Are you eating properly?' He looked quizzically at me, his pen hovering over the pad and a smile playing around his lips.

His smile transported me back to London. I always teased him about his quirky smile. It hadn't changed. It was a lovable smile that lit up his face and created little laughter wrinkles around the corners of his eyes. 'I try to eat properly, but sometimes I can't be bothered to cook.'

'Natural yoghurt is especially good if you are on antibiotics, but proper meals are essential. You should know that! I remember you as a health freak in London. You used to spend an inordinate amount of your stipend buying expensive fruits - and prawns of all things. You had weird tastes!' His face lit up and he threw me a warm, embracing smile. 'We had fun back then, didn't we? With all the fun we had, I don't know how we managed to earn our PhDs. My extended studies in Surgery and Tropical Medicine were horrendous.'

I smiled back. 'I think God was always on our side.' My mind flitted to our times in London. It was as if we were back in the pub across the street from our Halls of Residence, playing scrabble and arguing over correct spelling and allowable words. I usually won the game and although this didn't please him at all, he would shrug and say he would win the next round. He hardly ever did. I had been playing scrabble since I was a small child and my undergraduate years at Cambridge University had thoroughly equipped me with all the words in a voluminous Webster dictionary we used to sneak out of the library and faithfully returned each morning.

'Here is your prescription.' He reached for a desk calendar. 'I'd like to see you in ten days time when you've finished the antibiotics. Make an appointment with my secretary. Coughs and infections keep us busy this time of year and there may already be advanced bookings.'

Rather precipitously, I stood up, thanked him, and left the room. Having made the appointment with the secretary, I left the surgery and headed to the basement, feeling light-headed and carefree. For the first time in months, a surge of renewed life flooded my body.

The next ten days were busy ones for me. I had plenty of NGO consultancies to catch up on, but at the back of my mind was the thought that I would be seeing Richard again. I kept wondering how much he remembered our time in London. Did he remember it as much as I did? What was his home life like? Ten days later, I walked into his office. He looked up from the crossword he was doing, looked at his watch, gave me his quirky smile and asked in mock consternation, 'why do you like such early appointments? This is a little too early, isn't it?'

'I have a lot of things to accomplish, so the earlier I get my appointment over with, the better for me. At any rate, I hate visits to doctors.' I didn't sit down. He directed me to the examination room where the nurse took my blood pressure. She called him when she was done. As he poked me here and there with his stethoscope, he asked how I was feeling and I replied that my cough still persisted, but that the acute pain in my chest had almost disappeared. I told him I had faithfully followed his instructions and had been eating plenty of natural yoghurt, fruit and vegetables.

'Are you eating enough protein? You know proteins are the building blocks for the body. Let me see you in a week's time. By then your chest should have completely cleared up. If not, I may have to run a couple of tests. Get dressed and come to my office.' He walked out, pulling off the surgical gloves and throwing them into the bin.

I buttoned my blouse, put on my jacket, and joined him in his office. He was busy scribbling something on his medical pad. 'Have a seat.' I sat down and he continued writing. 'Continue to eat plenty of natural yoghurt to revamp your good bacteria.' Finally, he looked up. 'We are done for now, but make an appointment for any time next week.'

I thanked him, stood up, and headed towards the door.

'Are you leaving already?' he asked in evident surprise.

His reaction took me aback. 'We are done, aren't we?' I asked.

He flipped through his desk calendar. 'Since I have no patients this morning, I thought we could go for a cup of coffee. Do you have time?'

'That would be nice!' I exclaimed. I knew I was gazing at him with wide-open eyes because his invitation was so unexpected.

He burst into laughter and stood up. 'You look pleasantly shocked! Let's go.' He hung his white coat behind the door, slipped on his jacket and held the door open for me. 'I will be at Café Morocco if you cannot get me on the phone,' he told his receptionist.

We walked to the lift and went to Second Floor where there were several cafes and restaurants. Café Morocco was small and attractive. We opted to sit at a wide open space just outside the café at a corner table. I ordered coffee and a Danish pastry and he asked for tea and a slice of carrot cake. As we waited for our order, he asked me about my life and my husband. When I told him we had divorced years ago and that our only child was studying in America, he seemed genuinely distressed and asked what had happened. I shrugged. 'I really don't know; things just didn't work out. I guess he didn't love me enough or I didn't love him enough – c'est la vie. I really haven't figured it out. What about you? How many children do you have?' I was glad to divert attention from my bitter memories of my failed marriage.

'Two boys, two girls. The perfect number we planned to have. The firstborn is a boy aged sixteen, one daughter is almost fourteen, the other daughter is twelve and my last-born son is six years old. All well spaced.' He leaned back in his chair, staring hard at me.

Our order came. I stirred my coffee thoughtfully, my own action taking me back to countless cups of coffee and tea in our university rooms or in the pub in Bloomsbury Square where we played scrabble practically every evening after a day of exhausting lectures. We had a special corner in the pub, which the owner kept free for us on particular days. He often gave us free coffee and tea and sometimes snacks because he liked talking about Africa and all its problems!

'What does your wife do?' I asked, coming back to the present.

'She runs her own business.' He did not elaborate and I didn't ask him to.

'I guess you have a four-by-four vehicle and a beautiful house to booth' I said jokingly.

'Actually, I don't have a four-wheel vehicle because it has never crossed my mind to get one, but now that

87

you mention it, I shall definitely think about it. We live in a University house, but I have just started building ours. What about you?'

'I live in a rented house, but I have an upcountry house I am renovating.'

'Where is the upcountry house located?' He stirred his tea almost absentmindedly.

'It's near Warufaga, a high-altitude place which gets deadly cold from June to July.'

'You are joking! I pass close to that place when I go to check on my flower farm. Where exactly is your house?'

I pulled out a small notebook from my handbag and drew a map for him, pointing out landmarks, which he probably knew. He nodded as he recognized the landmarks. 'Next time you are in that direction, drop in and look at it. I keep a worker to take care of the place, so he can give you a cup of tea. Just tell him you are a friend of mine,' I offered generously.

We were getting into an animated discussion about our times in London, especially the great times we had in the parks, when his cell phone rang. 'I have a patient, so I have to return to my surgery,' he said, abruptly, as if he didn't want to talk anymore about our life in London. I wondered if he had suddenly remembered the short fling we had had.

'Thank you so much for the lovely time. I have really enjoyed myself. I am surprised you remember so much about our time in London,' I said, pushing back my chair to stand.

'It was good talking to you. We had good times in London, didn't we?' he said. 'See you next week'.

After he left, I took the lift to the Ground Floor where there was a florist shop. I felt so happy I decided to send him a bunch of flowers. I walked into the florist shop and looked around. There were beautiful orange roses in a huge bucket of water. I asked the florist to prepare a bouquet of them with Baby's Breath, while I looked for a card. I found a nice one, which seemed to express the thanks I felt. I paid for the bouquet, scribbled a 'thank you' in the card, addressed the envelope, and asked the florist to deliver the bouquet to his surgery. Later on, I called the receptionist to ask if the florist had delivered the flowers. She confirmed they had, thanked me and said they brightened the office.

When I went for my next appointment, I met his wife. I was in the waiting room reading the newspaper when she and Richard walked out of his office. Richard introduced us. She smiled at me and said, 'I saw photos of you when the two of you were students in London ages ago.' I noticed how extraordinarily attractive she was. Richard walked out of the door with her. When he returned, he asked me to step into the examination room where the nurse was waiting. My chest infection had fully cleared. After an examination, he invited me into his office.

'I visited your upcountry house and it is a fantastic place! In fact, I meant to stay just five minutes, but ended up staying for over an hour. It is a good investment. You could make a fortune planting roses for export. The grounds are large enough. Perhaps I should lease the place from you and increase my flower business. By the way, talking of roses, thanks for the beautiful ones you sent. No one has ever bought me flowers before.'

'Surely your wife has?' I asked with a frown on my face, remembering the many times I used to buy flowers for my husband.

He shook his head and laughed. 'She never has. It is really not part of our culture, is it?'

'All men deserve flowers as much as women do. I am glad you liked them. I enjoyed buying them for you.' I felt no embarrassment as I said this. I genuinely meant what I was saying. It never occurred to me that what I was saying was audacious or unacceptable.

'What do you intend doing with your house in Warufaga? It's is enormous.'

I explained that I wanted it to be a Guest House where visitors could spend weekends or holidays, but that it would take years to renovate it to the required standard.

'You will do it. Be patient. I know that once you decide to do something, you go for it full throttle.' He smiled encouragingly at me and placed his warm hand over mine, but quickly withdrew it.

Now, as I write this, a bolt of pain shoots through me. At this precise moment, I regret having lost Richard, not as a lover, but as a true friend, as my soulmate. He had become an integral, precious part of me. Through my windows, I stare at the mass of freshly fallen purple blossoms beneath the jacaranda trees. The exquisite sight heightens my pain. 'Life', I say aloud 'is difficult to understand, difficult to comprehend fully. Why is life is so pain-filled?' Hot tears cruise down my cheeks. I don't know why I am weeping. Since the break up, I cry so easily, especially when I think back to those moments I shared with Richard. My life has not been the same since we broke up. I truly lost a part of my heart. The missing part is a gnawing crevice which only Richard's presence can fill. He must return with the missing part and splice it onto my remaining fragment.

I force myself to remember exactly how the affair started. I force my memories to come together, forcing each piece to fit neatly into place. I want to create a meaningful picture. Bit by bit, I remember that exact day vividly. The images coalesce into one and become a single distinct image. In a flash, I remember everything as if the event took place just yesterday.

The day I met his wife, Richard had asked me to wait

for him in his office while he attended to two patients. When done, he had taken off his doctor's coat, hung it on the hook behind the door, looked at me with a smile and said we were going for coffee and a very long chat. We made our way to another more comfortable café, again choosing a corner table shielded by lovely palm trees in huge white ceramic containers. I was vibrating with happiness and I knew it showed on my face.

The next two hours flew by as we talked about all sorts of things: London, my house, his house, his farm, and the politics of our country. Apparently, we shared similar views on politics. We discussed the political situation in the country, the constant clamour for more accountability from our leaders, the blatant corruption ripping our country apart; the ever-sprawling slums, the unemployment and the wretched poverty. We talked about greedy government officials looting national resources instead of creating medical services, schools, and amenities for its citizens. We ended the discussion by hoping that our newly-elected Government would work hard towards addressing the ills of the past.

Our animated discussions reverted back to our time in London. He reminded me that whenever we got upset with each other, we would not talk to each other for several days, just like sulking children. We laughed at the memory. It seemed just yesterday. It was hard to believe that eighteen years had simply condensed into nothing but this moment. It was as if we were still carefree students. Yet, here he was, a Professor of Surgery at the University, a doctor with his own clinic, and a husband with four children. He seemed to have so much going for him. He was successful, while I was divorced, with my daughter in America, and still a struggling NGO consultant with a pathetic pay, which hardly made ends meet. Feeling devoid of meaningful accomplishments as I listened to Richard talk about his accomplishments, life and his dreams, I expressed as much to him. With discontent in my voice, I said that compared to him, I was a poor Church mouse.

'How can you say that? You are a recognized environmentalist and your NGO job sounds a good one. You bought your upcountry house cash and you have an urban plot you are in the process of developing. To me you seem pretty well off. Anyway, wealth isn't everything. Happiness is far more paramount,' he said quietly, twirled his teacup in its saucer.

'I guess you are right and I should stop complaining. There are people in our country who go to bed hungry every day.' I wondered how it was that we were able to talk as though the gap of eighteen years did not exist. How was it possible for all those years to dissolve into the present moment as though we had never parted, as though we were still carefree students discussing politics and getting into silly little quarrels?

As we were saying goodbye, he casually said he might pop in for a cup of tea when I was next at my upcountry house. His comment delighted me and I realized how much our friendship had meant when we were in England. I wanted to rekindle the special friendship we had shared. Later at home, I took out our college photographs and gazed at them as if looking for a message in them. I had an urge to call him. I fingered the phone, debating if I should call him. Reluctantly, I refrained from doing so, not wanting to overstep the boundaries. He was, I firmly told myself, a married man.

One morning, my mobile phone rang. It was Richard. He said he was going to his farm for the weekend and wanted to know if by any chance I was going to my upcountry house and if so, might he pass by that evening and have a cup of tea with me? Coincidently, I had been upcountry the whole week seeing to some renovation work. I told him he was welcome to come by. I decided to prepare a light meal just in case he wanted something to eat. He arrived around seven-thirty that night. I was both excited and anxious. After he had washed his face and hands, we had tea and discussed all sorts of topics. When he finished his tea, he kept looking at his watch. After a while, he said he had better get going since he did not want to be late getting to his farm which was several hours drive away.

'Is it safe for you to drive so late at night?' I asked. My concern was genuine; carjacking was rampant in the whole country and our particular area was particularly notorious, especially at night.

'I do it all the time and it is not too late yet. Thus far, I've had no problems.' He stood up.

I made a bolt decision and a torrent of words tumbled out. 'It's too late for you to travel to your farm. There are plenty of bedrooms in this house and the bed is made up in the spare room. You are welcome to stay.'

He was silent for some minutes. 'I think I'd better go. It isn't too late. Can I use your bathroom to wash my face? Cold water should do the trick.'

'You know where the bathroom is.' I handed him the towel he had used when he arrived.

He came out a few minutes later saying he felt refreshed. He asked for another cup of tea. I handed him the tea. He sipped it slowly. I felt was if each one of us was anticipating something momentous; as if waiting for the inevitable to happen, whatever that might be. The air was tense. We both fidgeted uncomfortably.

'I think I will accept your offer to spend the night here. By the time I get to the farm, it will be very late. So, shall I stay or have you revoked your invitation?' he asked with a laugh.

'You are welcome to stay. I honestly don't think it is safe to drive so late at night.' I had been genuinely concerned that he would insist on driving late at night. But who was I to worry?

"In that case, I might as well be comfortable,' he said, taking off his jacket. He removed his cell phone from one of the pockets and put it on the table. He refilled his tea mug and drank his tea slowly. When he finished, he leaned back on the sofa. I saw a wave of tiredness sweep across his face. The man looked totally exhausted. Empathy swept through my body. In a gentle voice, I suggested he go have a shower while I got supper ready.

'That sounds great. I am actually exhausted and a shower will revive me.' He slipped off his shoes and socks and followed me to the bathroom where I gave him a large beige towel.

'There are different types of shower gel so use whatever you want. If you need anything else let me know,' I said calmly. I felt as cool as a light breeze.

While he had a shower, I warmed the food I had cooked, made fresh salad and set the table. Early that morning, as is my habit, I had picked roses and put them on the dining table. I went to the spare bedroom, turned down the sheets, checked that the bedside lamp was working and laid out a *leso* and a couple of plastic hangers on the bed. I was glad that my worker had thoroughly vacuumed the carpet and room early in the morning. Everything looked neat and welcoming. Richard emerged from the bathroom looking refreshed and smelling of my lily-of-the valley shower gel.

'Thanks, that was great. I feel really, really refreshed. I remember how much you liked lily-of-the valley shower gel, so I used it,' he said as he entered the dining room where I was putting the last touches to the table. He bent down to smell the yellow roses.

'A hot shower is always welcome after a long safari. I can't believe you actually remember how much I love lily-of-the-valley shower gel. That is amazing. If you are ready, we can eat.' I sat down, indicating a chair across from mine.

'If you don't mind, I'll sit right next to you. At home, my kids insist on us sitting right next to each other so that we can eat from each other's plates.' He sat down and scooped salad onto his plate. 'I'll start with the salad. It looks good. I'm glad to see you are following your doctor's orders.' The lily-of-the-valley scent on his body wafted across my face.

Even as I write this, I am amazed at how we felt comfortable with each other after so many years apart. I realized that Richard and I had been real soulmates in London. No wonder that the pain of losing him as my friend is so unbearable. Perhaps if I continue to write about it, my pain will lessen, but as I resume, my heart constricts painfully. I want to reach out and touch his face, touch his velvety skin, listen to him and watch his quizzical smile light his face; I yearn to be with him; I ache to nestle within his encircling arms. I need him.

Back to that particular night. After dinner, I showed Richard the spare bedroom. 'I hope you'll not be too cold. There are spare blankets in the cupboard. Here's a *leso* in case you need one.' I pointed out the things on the bed. My heart started pounding for no apparent reason. I could feel it racing. I thought Richard must surely hear it pounding. What happened next startled me. Richard moved closer to me, wrapped his arms tightly around me and buried his head in my shoulders. The weight of his head made me realize in a flash that the man was exhausted and was in need of comfort. I pulled away, fear vibrating throughout my body.

'Please don't pull away from me,' he whispered.

'I need a shower,' I said, quickly wriggling out of his arms and making my way to my bedroom to get my nightgown and robe. I entered the bathroom and locked the door. My heart was racing so fast, I had to sit down on the bathroom stool. After I had calmed down, I stepped into the shower and ran hot water over my quivering body. I took some time to shower. When I emerged from the bathroom and went into my bedroom, I was shocked to see Richard reclining on my bed watching T.V. He had even lit the red candle on my nightstand. The candle bathed the room in a warm red glow and cast his shadow on the opposite wall.

'What are you doing here?' I asked. 'You can't sleep here, Richard, you can't!' I was almost shouting.

He switched off the T.V., pulled back the sheets and said 'get between the sheets before you catch another cold. I do not want to treat you with any more antibiotics. Come on, get into bed.'

'I am not sure if what you are doing is right,' I said in consternation.

'Just get into bed. All we are going to do is to simply talk, nothing more,' he said.

Gingerly, I got into bed. He blew out the candle, pulled me to him and nuzzled his head into my bosom. Slowly, gently, tenderly, he caressed me. I pushed him away, but he drew me to him. Surprisingly, I did not resist this time. As he caressed me, I remembered a dream I had had many months before I went to see him for my first appointment. I had dreamed that I had fallen in love with a married man. Now, here I was in bed with a married man! I hurriedly pushed away the nagging, troublesome thoughts that were flooding my mind.

I allowed him to draw me closer into his arms. I could feel his heart beating rhythmically. Mine was beating so hard, I thought he must surely hear it. We were both silent. I allowed his soft hands to explore my body. After a while, he began to talk very quietly, uttering soothing words, telling me to relax and not to be afraid. I tried to suppress my guilty feelings that what we were doing was wrong. As quickly as the thought crept into my mind, just as quickly I reasoned that I was not cheating on anyone since I was divorced, refusing to admit that I was in the process of aiding Richard to cheat on his wife. I shut my ears to my own inner protestations, arguing with myself that I deserved to be happy.

He said he wanted to comfort me and to show me that he cared; that he had heard the pain in my voice whenever we had had coffee in the city. Bit by bit, I felt my body loosen up, as if an invisible being was massaging my knotted muscles. I felt Richard's tenderness saturate my entire body. Slowly, slowly, he awakened my frozen feelings, expressing comforting, tender words. Before I knew it, we were making love. It was exhilarating and incredibly beautiful. For the first time, I experienced real ecstasy. Our chemistry matched perfectly. Once our inhibitions were thrown to the wind, we couldn't seem to get enough of each other. I thought I would die from the all-enveloping passion. We hardly slept that night.

The morning came all too soon. Richard wanted to leave as early as he could. I made him breakfast and he was gone by six a.m. I went back to my bedroom and slept like a baby for hours. When I woke up, I found several missed calls from him. Later, when he finally got hold of me, he said he had arrived safely and wanted to find out how I was feeling. Before I could respond, he said very quickly, 'it was incredibly wonderful. Thanks,' and switched off his phone.

As I attempt to write about this experience, I realize that I don't want to cheapen the wonderfulness of our intimacy by putting it down on paper. It is a precious memory best kept to oneself. As I write, I feel no remorse or guilt that my lover was a married man with a wife and children. At the time, I told myself that it was fate that brought us together. I could find no other explanation for it; how was it that for eighteen years we lived in the same city yet had never once run into each other? How was it that we had we made no effort to call each other? Now, eighteen years later, we were renewing our youthful friendship, completing what we had started.

Our meetings took on a certain rhythm and regularity that seemed perfectly natural. We never demanded anything from each other and never questioned each other about the lapses before our next meeting. Once, as we nestled in each other's arms, we discussed the brief fling we had had in London. We remembered we had broken it off because we had been worried about possible consequences. What if I got pregnant in the middle of my studies? More importantly, we both had partners back home. Whenever we talked about our student days, there was always a note of sadness, a note of nostalgia, in both our voices, as if unable to bridge the chasm across the years.

Early this morning, before I began writing, I looked out of the window and noticed that it was raining. I sighed heavily because my jacaranda trees would soon lose all their magnificent blossoms. Yesterday, as I drove through one highway, I enjoyed the swathes of frilly, lacy yellow cassia blossoms which intermingled beautifully with blue-purple jacaranda blossoms on the ground. The cassias are pretty, but they do not take away my breath as do the jacarandas which will always remind me of Richard. His face constantly interweaves itself between the jacarandas, my thoughts, and memories. This morning, I stood up, moved to the window and gazed out. I wanted to indulge in the beauty of the jacarandas, to feast my eyes on the thick carpet of fallen blossoms. This seemed the only way to assuage the pain the mauve-blue blossoms induce whenever I recall the break up after two years of exciting intermittent liaisons with Richard.

Initially, after several nights with me upcountry, away from his family, he started to worry that I might start to expect something more than a night here, a night there, a day here, a day there. I assured him I was not interested in breaking up his marriage.

Thereafter, we formed a habit of having coffee at various cafés, arranging to meet at my upcountry house whenever he went to check on his farm and at my town apartment whenever he could sneak away. Wherever the meeting took place, I would make tea and snacks or dinner and we would talk about a myriad of things. Politics dominated our conversations. We were both in agreement that Arab Springs-type revolutions were not the answer for Africa; wherever they had occurred, more problems inevitably followed. We were both of the opinion that our country was facing unimaginable individualism and elitism which had become dominant driving forces among our people; that our society had become a man-eat-man society; even human garbage scavengers fight daily for a share of dumping sites where they forage for food, clothing, trinkets, and waste paper for recycling as income generating activities; even demonstrating against eviction from such sites.

Each time we met, I was tempted to ask questions about his wife, but invariably held back, not wanting to invade his privacy. In the two years we were together, we hardly ever talked about her, yet we always talked about his children and their achievements. However, from bits of information gleaned here and there, I knew that his wife was not only brilliant in her profession but also a high achiever in her business ventures. As I got to know Richard better, I formed a picture in my mind that he was a family man who enjoyed taking his family out on weekends or for dinners. He didn't drink and he didn't go to nightspots with his friends. He was a hardworking doctor, husband and father; a man any woman dreams of having as a husband and father to her children; a reliable, solid family man. But if he was cheating on his wife, how reliable was he as a husband? 'With all this going for him, what is he doing with me?' I kept asking myself.

Several times I found myself fretting over him as if I were his wife, telling him he needed to be careful, that he was working too hard. When I saw that he didn't like me telling him this, I quickly put a stop to it. After all, he wasn't mine to fret over. Instead, whenever he told me how tired he was, I remained quiet for several long minutes before saying, 'let me massage the tiredness out of your body.' Even though I was genuinely concerned about his health and discerned that he needed time for himself, I knew it wasn't my place to intervene. However, each time he laid his head on my lap, I felt the tiredness ooze from his body and flood mine. Cradling his head in my arms, I would gently massage his taut temples, kiss him tenderly, teasing him that I was kissing away his worries and tiredness. Immediately, he would snuggle against me, draw me into his arms, and shush me to silence, as if he wanted to toss aside all his anxieties.

Now, in retrospect, I realize I actually got to know little about him in depth. I didn't get to know anything his friends and family. Yet, in his encircling warm arms, I laid bare all my deepest thoughts and concerns to him, telling him about my family, their likes and dislikes, their achievements and non-achievements. Even if he never met them in person, he already knew their entire histories from the times we spent together. At this moment, I rationalize that this is what we women do. It is as if we are driven by an inner force to lay our souls bare, as though we cannot hold back important information and anxieties about ourselves. We reveal our most intimate secrets to our men, as if they are listening keenly. But I know, in hindsight, that men are usually too engrossed in their own particular problems to actually listen to us women.

As I write, I pause to ask myself if all Richard actually needed was space from his wife; if all he needed was a woman to pamper him and soothe away his worries, frustrations, and perhaps even pain. Perhaps, I simply happened to be a convenient resting spot for his head; an expedient welcoming space in which he could rest peacefully. Perhaps, I happened to appear at the right moment when he was in desperate need of understanding, in desperate need of fulfilling sex. As these thoughts flash through my mind, I flinch in guilt, afraid that I am being unfair to Richard. No matter how much time has passed since we ended our relationship, I owe him loyalty; it would be wrong to doubt his feelings for me, even if he was always reluctant to express them.

Whenever we were together, I gave myself completely to Richard, hardly ever holding back. Frequently, he sent me short messages on my mobile simply asking where I was. If my response was that I was home in the city, he would send another one saying he would be with me in less than half an hour. If traffic was not bad, he usually got to me within fifteen minutes. After a quick shower, he would insist on undressing me, voicing his appreciation of my lingerie as he slowly caressed my body from my eyes, down my nose, and all the way down my legs. The time we spent together was always tender, playful, and loving. Despite the fact that the time was fleetingly brief, there was no hurry in the intimacy of embraces, in the intimacy and ecstasy of love-making. After my initial inhibitions, arising from my fear that I had become The Other Woman, he taught me to take it nice and slow; how to enjoy every aspect of lovemaking until we were both satisfied. After a blissful hour or more or less, he invariably had a quick shower and a cup of tea before he rushed away, almost precipitously, like a guilty, naughty boy. He always sent back a text to say he had arrived safely, to thank me and express how much he had enjoyed himself.

One evening, two years into the affair, very abruptly, he said in a low voice, 'it is untenable, isn't it? I am so terrified and terribly confused. I am getting too close to you, too close to think of stopping seeing you, but I am absolutely sure my wife suspects something. I am in real trouble if she does. Please, please, let tonight be our last night together. We have to break this chain around us or we shall both perish. She has begun to ask awkward questions. We have to break up.' His words flowed in a rush, in a muddled sort of way. He moved to my CD player, popped in a CD, drew me into his arms, and whispered, 'listen to the song and forgive me.'

The song was 'Let's Kiss and Say Goodbye' sung long, long ago by the Manhattans. With his arms around me, I listened and wept. He was quiet, but his silent warm tears on my chest indicated that he too was hurting. Before this, I had begun to notice telltale signs: our meetings started to reduce; he often abruptly cut the phone; other times he wouldn't answer his phone; and he had begun to give me lame excuses whenever he couldn't see me. I too had started to feel afraid that we were becoming too closer for our own good.

'Please forgive me,' he said in a low voice, cupping his hands around my face.

'There is nothing to forgive. I knew it was only temporary,' I said with a heavy heart.

We said goodbye with hurried kisses. He got into the car, drove away, drove back, jumped out of the car, took me into his arms, kissed me, got into the car, drove away, returned, took my face between his hands, kissed me hungrily, and left, but returned with a spray of jacaranda blossoms he had picked from the tree. He thrust them into my arms, told me to look after myself and drove away for good. My security guard asked if he should lock the gate or wait for *Daktari* to return. I told him to lock it. The man's face looked sympathetic.

I was convinced Richard would return; that he loved me enough to return; that I knew he *truly* loved me; that for sure, he would return. When he did not return, I told myself there must be a good reason why. All my calls to him went unanswered. I suspected that he had changed his number. I reasoned that he must have loved me in his own special way and that surely he would return. But as the weeks and months sped by, I knew, without anyone reminding me, that, when all is said and done, a man will not easily give up his wife and children for The Other Woman. He has invested too heavily in his family. These days, his wife would surely take him to the cleaners if he dared leave her.

Pain and anger made me ask my innerself stupid, difficult questions. Had he ever loved me or was it only sex he needed? Did he enjoy my company or did it allow him to forget his worries? Did he want to get away from his family and gruelling schedules? I remembered *the only time* I ever asked him to say he loved me, he said such words were not easy to say, that they had to come from deep within his heart. His bluntness made me turn away from him in evident distress and anger. Even when he attempted to make amends by caressing me, I withdrew into my deepest self, curling into a tight ball, not wanting his body to touch mine. Violently, I pushed him away; angry that he had the audacity to make love to me yet could not bring himself to utter 'I love you.' At the time, after long minutes of silence, he said, 'you are withdrawing into your cocoon again. Please don't do that. You know my situation. I don't want to give you any false expectations by uttering such words. Please, don't push me away.' There was panic and anguish in his voice. He reached for me almost frantically.

Thankful that my bed was king-sized, I moved farther away, curling myself into a ball, as tight as a well-inflated one. How could I move close to him when he had refused to express three words – I love you -? He reached for me, turned me around, unfolded my arms and drew me to his chest, encircling me with his arms so tightly I could not move; in fact, I was suffocating. I struggled until he released me, allowing me to move away. He left the bed and went to make himself tea.

Later, when enough time had passed, he got into bed, reached for me, stroked my face tenderly and kissed me again and again. Irrationally, I acquiesced to his gentle lovemaking, my anger forgotten. With his arms snugly entwined around me and his soft whispers of love in my ears, I fell asleep.

Earlier on, I put my pen down. With countless memories swirling all around me and my cup of coffee in my hand I made my way to the jacaranda trees. After a light drizzle and wind in the night, the blossoms lay scattered around the mother tree, looking like a blue carpet. They reminded me of fallen cherry blossoms in springtime in London. The sight evoked a sense of sadness within me; a feeling of indescribable loss. Stabbing pain cut me to the core.

I saw Richard's smiling face outlined against the mass of mauve-blue blossoms. What was it about him that turned my world upset down? Why do I still dream vividly of him? Vivid dreams in which I touch him, talk to him, and feel his arms around me? If I lived in West Africa, I would say he gave me powerful *juju* to bind me to him; he bewitched me beyond my rationality. Perhaps, he did use some sort of *juju* to bind me to him forever since I still crave his tenderness, his caring, and his appreciation for the tiniest details of our intimacy. I pine for his arms to encircle me. I hunger for the tenderness of his slow, unhurried, gentle lovemaking. I yearn for his whispered words of pleasure. I want to watch his quirky smile creep up and light up his tired face. I want to hear his soft laugh that used to make me as delighted as a happy, saliva-dripping puppy. I simply want to nestle within his loving arms and feel his heart beat softly in rhythm with mine.

Warm tears cruised down my cheeks. I returned to my desk, sat down and closed my eyes. A picture of our love emerged; at first, full of colour and light, bringing to mind tender, joyous moments, evoking the loveliness of jacaranda blossoms against the ever-changing African sky. But then the picture became a dull one of pain and regret, losing its vibrant luminosity, fading into a dull smudge, just like fallen jacaranda blossoms, which sadly, after a few days of rain, usually turn into an ugly purplish-grey mush.

Hastily, in my mind, I tore up the picture, my heart as heavy as sodden jacaranda blossoms. I broke into uncontrollable weeping for a few seconds. I sensed that something inexplicable had my purified my soul. I no longer felt sad. As calmness returned, I accepted that my pain would never disappear completely; there will be sudden moments when the memory of Richard will pierce my heart and turn my world upside down, whether for a fleeting moment or for hours or days or weeks. After all, he did take a slice of my heart as I did his, splicing his bit into mine.

I decided to paint a tangible picture, not one in my mind. I laid out my art materials and propped my stretched canvas on the easel. Staring intently at the bare canvas, I debated which colours to us. Should I use blazing reds to express the exhilaration of our love or should I use sombre reds to express the pain of it? Should I use yellows to convey the hope of it or should I use dull ochre yellows to convey the despair of it? Should I use mauve-blues and purples to capture the gentleness and the exquisiteness of it? As I pondered on the possibilities, the colours of the rainbow swirled about me, dazzling my eyes with their shimmering wonder. Quickly, I decided on the colours for my new picture. Methodically, I laid blobs of gleaming white acrylic paint on the palette. With a broad brush, I scooped the white paint and swept it across the canvas, back and forth, back and forth, back and forth, until the paint ran out. Squeezing more white onto the palette, I picked it up with the brush and rapidly whizzed the paint-loaded brush across the canvas until the surface vibrated with luminosity, with the shimmering white light of joy. Almost impatiently, I waited for the paint to dry completely, thankful that I was using acrylic paints instead of oils. As I waited, I closed my eyes, breathed very slowly, very gently, very thoughtfully, until I saw a clear image of Richard's smiling face in my mind.

Quickly, I laid out blobs of Prussian blue, ultramarine blue, cobalt blue, and magenta on another large palette. With the fingers of my right hand, I scooped up paint and created my lover's face in vibrant, scintillating mixtures of mauve-blues with shadows of deep purple for contrast. Forth and back, forth and back, my finger moved with lightning speed, a stroke here, a streak there, a dash here, and a squiggle there. Soon, my picture became tangibly alive, rich with mauve-blues and deep purples, abounding with life, and luxuriant with hope. The picture was perfect. Very, very, slowly, I took a deep breath, and with infinite love, murmured, '*I shall forever celebrate our togetherness with endless joy.*' I leant towards the picture and gently breathed into it the shimmering soul of my beloved jacarandas. Richard smiled happily back at me. I touched his face fleetingly, afraid to rekindle my anguish.

Immediately after, I walked slowly to one of my jacaranda trees, opened my arms wide and asked it to shower me with its bluest blossoms, beseeching it to soothe my soul with its deepest purple symphonies. It obliged me, promising that my pain will one day disappear forever. I wiped away my tears with a handful of velvety mauve-blue blossoms.

Later, when the evening sun turns the jacaranda blossoms into a wonder of scintillating purples, and my soul is calm, I will finally put on paper my story of joy and pain.

CHAPTER FIVE

Lucy

I had it all – mansions, real estate, cars, jewellery, designer clothing, designer toiletries, and *anything* and *everything* I could lay my hands on. I had children, a husband, chauffeurs, gardeners, domestic servants, personal assistants, beauticians, stylists. I had more shoes than Imelda ever had. I had twenty-four hours unparalleled security. For good measure, I had a young secret lover to brighten my mundane sex life. Yes indeed, I had everything, except a conscience, which, in my estimation, was a bothersome hindrance best pushed to the farthest reaches of my extravagant world.

Considering I had come from a poverty-riddled village home, I had climbed a mountain higher than Everest. My husband's ascendancy to the highest echelons of political power had catapulted me to unimaginable heights of grandeur and provided a bottomless goldmine for us, for our extended families, and for our perpetual bootlickers. I even had a salary! Parliament had decreed that the First Lady of the Republic deserved a decent salary for all the many public appearances she made such as visiting children's homes, hospitals and attending the occasional gathering of First Ladies of the region. My salary of half a million shillings was good pocket money for buying supporters and informers. I wasn't about to let my husband's presidency diminish and dissipate; he had to serve at least two terms, preferably longer through a little, gentle manipulation of the Constitution. I couldn't bear the thought of losing my vast fortunes. The world belonged to me and would only continue to be so if I played my cards right.

I trained myself to take on the demeanour of a hard-working First Lady of the Republic, ever ready to whip out my best smile and to exude an aura of goodness. In my own home, however, my tongue was razor-sharp; my temper a veritable *tsunami* that swept everyone and everything aside when it tornadoed out of my irate being. My monumental attitude and piercing eyes were capable of reducing annoying people to ant size. When my maid, or a stupid Member of Parliament, made the mistake of arousing my anger, my well-aimed slaps were as hard as those of the stereotypical upper-class Latino women featured in soap operas; women who constantly crack their maids' skulls with their fists and all manner of weapons. If these rich upper-class women could be so uncouth, so uncivilized and so devoid of human kindness, yet still emerge winners after reciting prayers to their Madonna, perhaps I could borrow a leaf or two from them. I considered that while these soap opera characters had the manners and language of undesirable coyotes and skunks, mine was less abusive and I did have a little milk of kindness in my heart. I actually wept over the fate of our poor, disadvantaged children, especially the orphans.

I had learned that political expediency requires one to have a ready well of tears to draw from when confronted by glaring, suspicious, impoverished people who hang on to every word spoken by politicians and those in power. I had quickly learned the tricks of the trade and my tears had stood me in good stead many a time. I was fortunate to have bodyguards who accompanied me wherever I went – sometimes insisting on accompany me to the doors of the ladies' in public places to make sure I was not kidnapped! They shielded me against danger. I hardly ever stopped to count my blessings since it was perfectly natural that the good things of life should come my way. After all, hadn't I suffered when I was growing up? Hadn't I walked barefooted to our jigger-riddled school? Hadn't I undergone FGM to make me a worthy wife to a man some day? And as the First Lady, didn't I visit countless children's homes and hospitals? Didn't I attend numerous public rallies to sing my husband's achievements and promises of a better life for all and to prove that behind every successful man there is a vigilant woman?

Whenever I sat at my dressing table in the mornings and looked at myself in the mirror, I bristled with a sense of accomplishment, a sense of my own unbelievable political dexterity and ingenuity. I was a monumental First Lady. My husband relied on my advice and good judgement. Bed time was an opportunity for me to give him free advice he so badly required. He gave into my desires and whims until my bank account and property portfolios were bulging, threatening to bust at the seams. A leading foreign publication had reported that I was the fifth richest black woman in Africa. It irked me that I wasn't yet at par with that famous female African-American multibillionaire reputed to be the first richest Black media mogul and philanthropist. I told my husband he had better see to it that my bank accounts started to swell or else I would reveal all his unsavoury secrets! I saw him literally quake in fear.

Then BWOW! The unimaginable happened. A cyclone of monumental proportions hit us, turning our world upside down. My own world fell apart. Things happened at such an incredible speed, the whole nation was left aghast with disbelief and with properties and lives up in smoke. We had just stood up for the National Anthem at one of our National Holidays when rapid gunshots rang out. I saw my husband clutch his chest and reel backwards. I heard Cabinet Ministers next to us scream and collapse to the ground, blood spewing everywhere. I felt searing pain in my chest and saw a million stars before blackness engulfed me. I fell to the ground.

I woke up to brightness, to a squishy, buoyant type of warmth. I stood up and was soon walking along a tree-lined avenue, humming quietly, happily. I felt an invigorating, fresh, pure breeze sweep across my face. I inhaled the clean air. Everything around me looked pristine. I walked along leisurely, in no hurry at all, until I came to a tree right in the middle of the road. It looked like a Tree of Life I had seen in Indian and Persian miniature paintings. The tree was loaded with luscious, iridescent fruit, which resembled my sparkling diamond and ruby necklaces. I picked a fruit and bit into it. Sweet juice oozed into my mouth. Ravenously hungry all of a sudden, I picked a second one. The flavour was deliciously different. I picked a third one. The taste was between a ripe apple, a banana, and sun-ripened mango. I popped a couple into my pockets, planning to plant the pips of these unusual fruit trees in my upcountry farm.

I continued walking, humming softly, humming happily. Before long, I saw a lake to my right. It reminded me of Lake Naivasha where I had a lakefront mansion, a kickback gift from an American billionaire who, through my efforts, had won a tender to supply military hardware to our Government. Over several nights of whispering sweet nothings into my husband's half-alert ears, I had managed to persuade him to accept nothing less than a 10 percent kickback for himself, a 5 percent for his Finance Minister, and a little place for me in Naivasha with its sparkling freshwater lake and lovely spreading acacia trees. For good measure, I asked for a tiny apartment in Florida near one of my rich friends who had conveniently exiled herself to the States after the change of Government, which had brought my husband, her husband's bitter rival, to power. Having been a beneficiary of the previous Government, she had not wanted to be asked any questions about her wealth by the newly revamped Kenya Revenue Authority whose tentacles could reach all the way to China and beyond. With a broad smile and the tender under his groaning belt, the American billionaire had given me the titles and keys to both properties.

I walked towards the shimmering lake and sat down on the lovely, soft grass. I gazed at the inviting blue water, wishing I had learned to swim. It occurred to me that I had no clue where I was heading to. 'Where am I?' Surprisingly, I was not in the least bit worried. I realized I had seen neither human beings nor animals, although where I looked I saw plenty of twittering birds and colourful butterflies. I stood up and continued walking, following a road that meandered gently through a variety of trees, some with bright green leaves and others with red-gold leaves. There were thousands of jacaranda trees all ablaze with their purple blossoms.

Finally, I arrived at an ornate gate, richly gilded with glittering specks of gold and silver. I peered through the grills and called out. No one answered. I reached for a switch mounted on the marble wall and pressed it. The gates slid open. As I passed through, they closed behind me. In the distance, I saw a gleaming white mansion. As I approached the mansion, I wondered where I was. 'This must be Europe. How did I get here?' I wondered. I rang a bell outside a door.

The door opened and a young woman emerged carrying a slick laptop. She glanced at me and said, 'I have been expecting you Mrs. Maringo, come right in.'

I followed her into a huge sunlit courtyard bordered with flowers of all shapes and colours. The lawn was a lush, vibrant green. The young woman walked briskly ahead of me, leading me to a glass door at the farthest end of the courtyard. When we got to the door, it slid open and we walked through into a huge reception area.

'Mrs. Lucy Maringo, newly arrived,' she announced to the elderly man at the counter.

He glanced briefly at me, then at the screen in front of him. He touched a few buttons here and there and frowned at the young woman. 'Her name's not here,' he said.

'It's on my screen,' said the young woman, popping open her laptop.

He touched a few buttons on his gleaming computer. 'First name and last name?'

'Lucy Maringo,' said the young woman.

'Ha! Found her. Take her to Timothy. He will sort her out.'

'Follow me, Mrs. Maringo.' She walked fast down a long corridor.

I followed her until we came to another desk where an elderly man was seated. My guide said in a clear voice, 'Timothy, this is Lucy Maringo, newly arrived.'

The man at the desk didn't hesitate. 'We've been expecting her. I shall take it from here. 'Follow me, Mrs Maringo,' he said, standing up. He was extremely tall and lanky.

I followed him to another door. It slid open. We walked through to a brightly lit room.

'Gabriel, this is Mrs Lucy Maringo, newly arrived,' announced Timothy.

'Thank you, Timothy, you can return to your work station,' Gabriel said in a quiet voice.

Timothy left the room. I gazed at Gabriel who did not invite me to sit down. His face was indistinct, blurred by a bright light, which shone all around him. I blinked several times in an effort to see him better. Why did the silly man not want to be seen?

'You have to go back home, Lucy,' Gabriel said, as though I had refused to do so.

'Where am I?' I asked. A sharp shaft of pain shot

113

through my chest.

'There was a coup d'état in your country. You were shot. Your husband and several others were killed.' said Gabriel in a calm, unconcerned and unhurried voice.

'Did my husband die?' I asked, wondering if Gabriel had been one of my husband's security men.

'Yes and so did you,' said Gabriel.

Disbelief swept through me. I began to laugh hysterically. 'You silly man! Why are you playing games with me? Don't you know I am the President's wife?'

'I am aware of that. You need to return home.'

'Where are my bodyguards?' I shrieked, looking frenziedly around me.

'A couple are dead and a couple are in hiding from all we have been able to gather,' said Gabriel without the slightest hint of sympathy in his voice.

I burst out laughing again. 'I will soon come out of this ridiculous dream,' I said.

'You are not in a dream. It's time for you to return home.' His voice sounded far.

I sat on a nearby sofa. It was warm and comfortable. A feeling of contentment flooded my being. I didn't want to go anywhere; I just wanted to sleep. I leant back and closed my eyes.

'Stand up, Lucy. It's time for you to go home. Tabitha will accompany you. Tabitha, show her the way home.' Gabriel's voice sounded suddenly harsh.

I felt someone's arms around me. 'Come along, Lucy.' She took my hand, pulled me to my feet, led me to a large room and pushed me onto a sofa. She pointed to the wall in front of me. A gigantic screen flickered to life. Bit by bit, I saw my entire life unfold from my birth to my death. The film of me was gruesome, unpleasant, and unsavoury. 'Stop it!' I yelled. 'Turn it off!' My cries echoed and re-echoed across the vast room. I was suffocating. 'Where are my bodyguards? Where are the children?' I screamed. The screams reverberated all around me.

'Stop screaming, Lucy. Come on, let's go home now.' Tabitha's voice was soothing.

'Are you a nurse? Am I in hospital? My whole body is sore. I am in terrible pain. Give me painkillers.'

'Follow that road straight ahead. It will lead you home. Bye!' Tabitha said, her words trailing her as she disappeared out of sight.

Darkness swirled around me. I felt I was falling through space. Suddenly, I landed with a thud on the biggest garbage dumpsite in our capital city. Gingerly, I stood up and picked my way through the putrid, evil-smelling sludgy mess. Nearby were human scavengers laughing and talking in strident voices. Gingerly, I approached them and heard a man say in a loud voice, 'that woman was dumped here several evenings ago. I think she might have been shot because she is covered in blood. She might die of infection if someone doesn't take her to a clinic.'

'I was here when she was brought in a pick-up and dumped over there. If indeed she was shot, then I am surprised she hasn't already died,' said a woman in filthy, smelly rags.

I was standing next to them yet they were talking as if I did not exist.

A man glanced my way. 'We should call the police to take her to a hospital. She needs to be checked if she was shot. She is covered in blood.'

Another woman said in a clear voice, 'it's none of our business. We had better leave her alone. I don't want to get into trouble or be asked any stupid questions by the police.'

In a clear voice, I asked why they were talking about me as if I did not exist. 'I am the President's wife. Why are you talking about me? If you say I was shot, who shot me?'

A loud voice piped up. 'She is crazy to say she is the President's wife! I guess she doesn't know that a coup took place. She is surely out of her mind if she imagines she is the President's wife!'

'If she is crazy, that is her business. After all, none of us, including you Patrick, is any better than she is.' The woman approached me. 'My name is Selena. What is yours, Mama?'

'I am the wife of the President! Where are my body-guards?' I was beginning to lose my temper. I stepped a few paces back because the woman's stench was so disgusting I felt like vomiting.

Selena took my hand in her grimy one. 'Don't be afraid to tell us your name, Mama.'

I pulled away from her. 'I am Lucy Maringo, the President's wife. What am I doing at this filthy dumpsite?' My head was reeling and I felt thirsty. 'Will you help me get home? I will pay you well and if you want a job, I will employ you in State House.'

More people surrounded me, some laughing loudly. 'She is completely nuts!' said a man.

Selena smiled pityingly at me. 'Mama, we all imagine strange things when we are a little sick in the head. Don't worry, I will help you. Since you are new to this dumpsite, feel free to ask me for help anytime. I'll show you how to collect sellable items. When you've made enough money, you can pay me something small for whatever assistance I will give you.' She drew closer to me and I stepped back as her putrid, evil-smelling scent assailed my nostrils. I retched and turned aside to vomit. I longed for my expensive French perfume to cleanse the foul air.

'Are you listening to me, Mama? I said I would help you. Do you want my help or not?' asked Selena, look-ing at me with aggrieved eyes.

I remembered the many times I had sped past this same dumpsite on my way to some function or other in Eastlands. I was always disgusted at the sight of the hordes of filthy, hungry people feverishly scavenging for whatever they could find to sell or to eat. Once or twice, I had asked my husband, the President, if the Government couldn't do something about this appalling place, but he had simply shrugged and said it was up to the Ministry concerned to deal with the matter. I had tried to suggest one or two programmes that could be put into place to help these people, but nothing ever materialized.

I moved away from Selena and vomited another stream of repellent bile as the repulsive smells threatened to choke me. Quickly, I touched Selena's my arm. 'I really am the President's wife. Please help me to get home.' Hot tears of extreme fear pricked my eyes.

'Don't you know that the President and some Ministers were killed several days ago? Who brought you to this dumpsite?' asked Selena.

'I remember my husband was shot, but I am not quite sure if it was true or not. Please help me to get home!' I clutched her arm tightly, afraid she might leave me.

The woman laughed raucously. 'Patrick, you are right. The woman is surely nuts. She keeps claiming to be the President's wife! At this rate, we will not be able to help her.'

'I told you so she is nuts, didn't I?' The man burst into loud laughter.

The rest of the horde drew closer to me and poked me here and there as if to test if I was human or not. Their faces were grey with filth and grime and their bloodshot eyes made me cringe in terror, terrified they would harm me. A couple of urchins stepped closer to me, their bottles of glue stuck to their noses, and stinking horribly. Their eyes were glazed, unfocused and dead-looking. I moved a few paces back from them.

'This woman is insane. Eti yeye ni wife ya Prezo!' exclaimed one urchin, laughing loudly.

A man stepped towards me and said a piercing, aggressive voice, 'mama, my free advice is for you to stop pretending to be the President's wife. If you continue making such silly statements, people will lynch you. Do not annoy us with your stupidity.'

'I am the President's wife, you dim-witted man!' I screamed, ready to give him a hard slap. 'As soon as my security men get here, they will teach you a lesson you will never forget!' I shook my fist at him.

Selena dragged me aside, a distance from the rest of the people who had gone back to their scavenging. 'Mama, if you continue abusing people, they will beat you up. If I had a full-length mirror, you would see for yourself that you are as filthy and bedraggled as the rest of us. I am not sure how you got here, but now that you are actually here, it is wise to befriend people here because some of them can be mean. If you want to stay here, I will teach you how to survive. I will show you how to find good food in this dumpsite. You can even find unopened packets of delicious fruit juices. Once you get the hang of things, you will find that there's plenty to eat if you know how to look for it. I will show you where we take garbage for recycling. I will even show you how to make a little place where you can live.' She came closer and whispered, 'you must always be on your guard against rapists. This place is full of them.'

Terrified, I said pleadingly, 'please believe me, I am truly the President's wife. I am sure my security men will arrive any time soon looking for me.'

Selena pinched me hard on my cheek and said angrily, 'look at yourself, you thick-headed woman! Which President's wife would be as filthy as you are? And if indeed you had security men, why did they let you out of their sight? If you continue to act foolishly, I will leave

118

you here alone to deal with these people. They may not be as kind as I am. I don't even know why I am being kind to you! And how many times do you have to be told that the President is dead?' There is even a curfew and we have to inside our hovels from six in the evening to six in the morning. Take a good look at yourself and tell me if you think you are truly the President's wife. How did you get so much blood on your clothes?'

I glanced quickly at myself and noticed that my designer outfit was tattered and covered in blood and unimaginable nauseating muck. I moved close to Selena and whispered desperately, 'I think I was shot. I am in great pain. And I am telling you the truth that I am the President's wife. Please help me to get out of this place. I don't want to stay here with half-wits.'

Selena clicked her tongue in annoyance. 'I am trying to help you stay out of trouble and here you are calling us half-wits. I ask you, is that gratitude?' She puckered her face in evident anger, took a deep breath and said in a patronizing tone, 'it's perfectly all right if you want to imagine you are the President's wife. Sometimes, we all have illusions of grandeur, don't we? Now and then, I too love to imagine I am the Queen of England because I have seen pictures of her in magazines that we often find in this dumpsite. When I am feeling unhappy over my fate and impoverished state, I like to imagine that this hellhole is my gleaming palace full of amazing treasures and that one day, I shall live in a palace. For now, I have no option but to call this place my home. If you like, I will take you to my carton dwelling over there. You will see how pretty it is inside. I found some good things in the dumpsite to decorate it. I even have a mattress, a sofa and a glass table! You can live with me until you have constructed your own place.'

I felt like wringing her neck that she did not believe that I was the President's wife. In exasperation, I said I was going home and began to stride away.

Selena grabbed me by the arm. 'Mama, if you leave this dumpsite, I assure you the police will arrest you and take you to a mental hospital because you are filthy and you sound mentally unstable. I warn you, many people from this dumpsite have ended up at that mental hospital. Soon after I arrived at this dumpsite I too was taken there for a few weeks, but I escaped. At this dumpsite, we only survive by sticking together and caring for each other. It is impossible to survive on one's own in this place. I am willing to help you because I feel sorry for you. It is possible that your relatives dumped you here because they didn't want to take care of you because of your mental state. We know of such cases, including one of a professor from the University whose relatives dumped him here when he became mentally ill. Probably, he would be dead or still living here if good Samaritans and newspaper reporters had not come to rescue him. Can you believe that those wicked relatives abandoned him here stark naked?'

Unbelievingly, I stared at Selena as she came to a stop. I trembled in great fear, not knowing whether or not to believe her stories. 'Are you telling me the truth about the Professor?'

Selena nodded. 'There are many stories to tell about this place and the people who find their way here. Now, as for you, if it is true you were shot you might die of infection if a doctor does not see to your wound. And even if you were not shot, perhaps someone knifed you because your clothes are caked with blood. Furthermore, perhaps you haven't notice, but your arm is dangling in a funny way as if it is broken. I can take you to a nearby clinic for treatment.'

'Is it true there was a coup in the country?' My head had unexpectedly become lucid.

'Yes and the new government is a bad military one.

They are hunting down and jailing the ex-President's sympathizers and supporters. But as you know, our President was a very bad dictator, so perhaps he deserved what he got. You had better stop rattling on about being the President's wife because there might be sympathizers of the military here.'

Hesitantly, I asked, 'might you know what happened to the President's family?' I waited with bated breath to get some news about my family.

'Oh, by now they have surely fled the country! We heard there were convoys of cars heading to the airport just before the coup and soon after. Others say that members of the previous Government rushed to the harbour to look for ships leaving for Europe and China.' Selena stepped close to me and said conspiratorially, 'you must be very careful what you say around this place, there are many spies listening keenly. People say the military is going to hand over to the Deputy President who was away in China when the coup took place.'

I wanted to box Selena's ears and tell her that I was present when the President and the Deputy President were shot. I saw the Deputy President collapse right in front of my eyes. Where did the rumour spring from that the Deputy President was in China?

'Why are you looking so thoughtful, Mama? Do you know something I don't?' Selena shook my arm vigorously. 'You suddenly look quite normal. Perhaps you aren't mentally unstable after all.'

'It is a lie that the military will give power to the Deputy President. He was not in China, but at the stadium with my husband the President. I saw both of them shot. I think they are both dead,' I whispered.

'Oh, no, not again! Not your stories again, Mama! What is wrong with you?' Selena glared crossly at me, but then her eyes lit up with kindness. 'Once we get to the clinic, the doctor will help you.'

I gazed intently at Selena, wondering how to convince her that I was not mentally ill and that I was truly the President's wife. In my lucidity, I shuddered at the enormity of my terrible predicament, trembling at the thought that my children might have been killed and if not, that they were worried to death over my whereabouts. 'Please walk to the road with me so that I can find a taxi to get home. Please help me,' I implored Selena, desperate to get out of this dumpsite.

'How many times do I have to tell you that in your state, the police will arrest you? Even if I explain that you are trying to get home, they will either ignore us or cart you off to God knows where! Since the coup, the whole country is unsafe. None of us dares to venture out of this dumpsite. Strangely, this is a safe refuge because no one bothers about human scavengers like us. This is a safe place for you.' There was no trace of mockery in Selena's voice. In her eyes, I saw genuine concern for me. 'The others are coming back. Be careful what you say. Come, let us sit under this jacaranda tree and you can tell me more about yourself.' Selena said, dragging me by the hand to the jacaranda tree which was in full bloom. 'Wait here for me. I will return soon. Be careful of what you tell people, Mama, and don't show them that you are afraid of them otherwise you will not be safe here. Only the fearless can survive in this place.'

Trembling in fear at being left alone, my strained eyes followed Selena as she strode away. In trepidation, I watched a group of human scavengers pick their way through the garbage towards me.

A surge of desperation, of entrapment, of complete helplessness, suffused my whole being. I heard an alien voice erupt from deep, deep within my soul. I heard it cry out, 'My God, my God, why hast Thou forsaken me?'

The only answer was the reverberating laughter of the human scavengers advancing towards me.

CHAPTER SIX

Esmeralda

Ominous. Menacing Ominous. Menacing. Ominous. Menacing. The words chase each other in my mind, each fighting to occupy a special niche. They scare me, evoking a mishmash of memories and distorted images. *Menacing. Ominous. Menacing. Ominous. Menacing.* In my restless mind, the words beat a rhythm all their own; similar yet distinctive. Hypnotically, like a guru reciting a mantra, I sway to the rhythm of the words. Unexpectedly and abruptly, the words leave my mind. But instead of relief flooding my mind at their departure, my restlessness returns.

I fidget uncomfortably in my wheelchair, my wrinkled, knotted hands clutching tightly to its cold aluminium supports. Old age is a terrible nuisance. *Ominous. Menacing.* From their prison deep in my mind, ghosts leap to life. I watch them flee down to the beach and plunge into the Indian Ocean. Furtively, painfully, I glance over my shoulders, expecting to see others lurking in the afternoon shadows, flitting here and there; dancing annoyingly in front of my tired eyes. I know they want to play with me, to tease me, to mock me; bent on reminding me that I am a lonely, wizened old woman who, rightfully, should already be six feet under the sandy soil of my coastal garden.

Ominous. Menacing. The words return, weaving their way in and out of my mind; horrible, borrowing, niggling little worms beleaguering me endlessly. Two other ugly words join them - *reduced circumstances*; two words with enough force to set me ablaze with indignity.

123

I stare past the lush lawn to the sea, an expanse of tropical turquoise lit by the late afternoon sun into a shimmering marvel. The ever-changing greens and blues of the sea are a feast for my tired eyes. The blues remind me of my violet-blue eyes. I pick up the mirror Agnes always thoughtfully places on the table next to my wheelchair. Even in my old age, I still possess a good dose of vanity. Whenever I look into the mirror, I see that I still possess surprisingly sparkling, vivid eyes; eyes too young for my advanced age.

I raise my head to look at a framed photograph on the wall opposite me. A young woman stands on a coral cliff waving her hands high in the air, her blond hair blowing in the wind. Before her is the wide, wide stretch of the Indian Ocean with frothy waves rolling in. Even though the photograph is turning sepia with age, in my mind's eye, the original colours are as vibrant as they were the day Albert took my picture. The young woman is vivacious with smiling red lips and laughing blue eyes. I was a real beauty then. And perhaps I still am! Oh, darling Albert, why aren't you here to authenticate that fact? Why aren't you here to help me while away the time with animated conversations? Why did you leave me alone in this world? Why didn't we depart together to that new world where you surely must be missing me?

Squinting against a shaft of light from the sea, I take a quick survey of my lovely garden. It is beautiful, exotic; a veritable paradise of tropical trees, shrubs and flowers. My wide curving veranda overlooks the Indian Ocean with its blues and emerald greens. Dear Albert always said my parents must surely have named me for the emerald greens of tropical seas. At both sides of the veranda, towering coconut trees and assorted palms provide, to use my eccentric architect's ostentatious words, *verticality* against the *horizontality* of the wide lawn and the expansive seascape beyond. Flamboyant trees, ablaze with flame-orange orchid-like blossoms, fling their spreading arms protectingly over the lawn, which, when freshly mowed, is a soft resilient carpet, soft to the touch, delightfully cool and soothing to sweaty feet on a sweltering tropical day. It is wonderful to fling off smelly flipflops or sandals and wriggle one's toes into the coolness of the grass.

Of all my trees in my charming garden, the most perfect is the jacaranda tree, which, several days ago, burst into a mass of mauve-blue bell-shaped blossoms. For the past two weeks, the jacaranda's leaf-less skeletal frame has been heralding our short rains. And sure enough, the first gentle drizzles arrived yesterday afternoon.

Over the years, and countless times, my faithful jacaranda has filled me with unspeakable joy and many times with throbbing sadness when I have felt utterly alone in the world. How many times, in earlier years, didn't I weep when I had to ask the gardener to prune some of its branches to give it more strength and better shape? How many times haven't I laughed with happiness under its shady arbours? How many times haven't I sat under its canopy and wept tears of desolation? And in all the years, not once has it complained, not once has it rebuked me for expecting so much from it. Instead, it has quietly listened to me; silently laughed with me; silently sung with me.

I wonder if it remembers that I brought it as a seed, amongst many others, more than thirty years ago from my upcountry home in Njoro and planted it at its exact spot at our new beach home. Does it recall that it was the only jacaranda seed that survived from at least ten others? God knows why, but the seed germinated, sprouted and struggled through human hands, sun, and rain to become a vigorous splendid tree.

My tired old eyes dart from one shrub to another; from one tree to another; from flowers to more flowers.

Before my confinement to my wheelchair, I was an avid gardener; gloves and secateurs always within easy reach. Yes, my garden is beautiful. Sudden joy warms the cockles of my heart. I sigh in relief as the bothersome ghosts disappear, leaving me to listen to the melodious woo-woo-wooing of the sea, and the booming sound of waves crashing against the coral outcrops to the far right of our beachfront. The woo-woo-wooing seems more mournful today than yesterday when it was soft and soothing, lulling me to peaceful, intermittent naps.

I reach for my diary, eager to put down all I am experiencing. Thankfully, despite my knotted fingers, I am still able to write! God only knows why, but I have always enjoyed scribbling down aspects of my life. My wheelchair has a sliding portion I can pull out for eating and writing on. I slide it open, pick up my hard-covered diary and begin to record my thoughts.

It is now late afternoon. The tide is coming in. Soon, the waves will come rolling in, pound the distant coral reef, and smash against the beach and coral outcrops with a loud booming sound. I watch the distant waves gradually build up. The sound of their breaking against the beach fills me with longing; longing to leap out of my confining wheelchair; longing to dash across the lawn to the beach; longing to plunge breathlessly into the incoming waves; longing to feel the sudden, tingling coldness of the water against my sweaty body. I crave to taste the saltiness of the water and feel it sting my eyes. The yearning gnaws deep within me. My old muscles pull and contract, pull and contract, pull and contract, as I attempt to get out of the wheelchair. Defeated, I flop back, a suffocating, constricted detainee.

Suddenly, a thought shoots through my entire body that I might die any minute now. I gasp in fear.

I struggle to breathe until deep, gasping breaths escape my lips. The idea that I might go anytime soon makes me shudder as if a cruel, biting wind has lashed my face, leaving painful welts across it. I put down my pen, pick up the hand mirror and glance into it, afraid I might indeed see raised welts across my face. Instead, I see my same wrinkled face and glints of sadness sparkling in the corners of my eyes. Feeling foolish at my own self-pity, I brush away my tears. Silly, silly old woman!

Regret and sorrow stab my heart. Regret for loss of vitality; loss of youthfulness; loss of meaning. Regret and sorrow that I am without kin in a foreign land I have called home for more than half a century. But it is home.

Images and memories flood my mind. There I am; a happy, carefree young bride enjoying life to the full with her husband in India; savouring every minute of the good colonial life in the age of the British Raj! There I am, a mere slip of a girl, instructing grown-up Indian servants to do my imperial bidding; sulking and pouting when things didn't go my quirky way. I recall how silently, they carried out my imperial orders.

There I am, hurriedly packing up, leaving our beloved India three years after it gained its hard-won *independence*; making our way by cruise liner to the port of Mombasa, to Kenya, our new colonial paradise; land of the Happy Valley lot with their notoriety talked about from one end of the British Empire to the next. Memories tear through my mind –building our 'upcountry' home at Njoro in the White Highlands where we grew wheat for twenty years before moving to the Kenyan coast to a dairy farm in Kuruwitu, a veritable paradise with private pristine beaches. The Mijikenda people, with their fascinating history and beliefs, became our neighbours and workers. Without them, we could never have survived the hardships of dairy farming!

In my wildest young dreams, I never imagined I would leave my nondescript English life, live in India and end up living in Kenya, first in the beautiful high-lands very similar to Devon, and then on an African tropical farm stretching all the way down to the beach. With the departure of more and more British settlers after Kenya's independence, properties, including beach ones, were sold at throw-away prices. Lucky us to have acquired a productive farm with a beautiful herd!

My mind races with colourful images of adventure-filled safaris in Kenya, sundowners, parties galore with the rest of our colonial ilk. Once settled at the coast, we hosted endless spectacular barbecue parties on our beachfront. What a glorious time we had!

Abruptly, an agonizing image of my beloved Albert in a coffin ten years ago replaces my happy images. Albert left me entirely alone in Kenya; no children, no relatives. Despite friends and my solicitor urging me to return to England, I was adamant that Kenya was my home. Thank God for my faithful staff!

A sudden pelting coastal downpour echoes my gloomy, pensive reflections. I stare at the sea, fast becoming a raging undulating mass of rising and falling grey waves of the incoming tide. The vibrant foliage of coastal shrubbery becomes dull; the brilliance of the sky quickly dissipates into an ominous, menacing drab haze. *Ominous. Menacing.* The bothersome words return to plague me; niggling worms weaving in and out of my strained mind. Out of nowhere, whirling dervishes join them to further plague me. *Ominous. Menacing.* I shiver as if I have caught a fever. The thundering sound of the ocean becomes irritating, menacingly, ominously oppressive. I close my eyes, breathing slowly to calm my nerves. Once calm and collected, I pick up my diary and slowly note down my thoughts.

The wind increases in volume, vehemently thrashing the palm fronds, which dance wildly sideways, down-wards, upwards; in a mad frenzy that leaves me in a hypnotic daze. The grey-white foam atop the rolling waves becomes voluminous, like white candyfloss tossed here and there by angry gods. Something about the waves reminds me of Greek myths. I see water nymphs riding the frothy waves; see Neptune leap out of the ocean in his gold-gilded throne and ride the waves with his nymphs. 'Neptune! Wait for me! Wait for me, Neptune!' I scream in a feeble voice which hardly carries far. Again, I try to wiggle my frail body out of the restrictive wheelchair. 'Neptune! Wait for me! Wait for me!' I put my diary and pen down and reach out my arms towards Neptune. He does not answer me but I see him wave back and disappear with his entourage beyond my gaze. My head flops back against the pillow Agnes unfailingly places behind my neck. What would I do without my dear Agnes?

The slow, steady drip-drop of the leaking corrugated iron roof begins. Drip-drop! Drip-drop! Drip-drop! The sound infuriates me and seething rage begins to suffuse my entire body. Ordinarily, I would have rejoiced to see and smell the rain; mild or heavy rain, it doesn't matter; rain has always been a soothing requisite to lull me into restful catnaps and deep, peaceful sleep. But now it incenses me, turning my mind into a smouldering cauldron of racing angry thoughts and images. The sound of the pelting rain and my ignited mutterings merge into a continuous cacophony of muted pain and deep resentment. I clench my fists angrily at the thought of my helplessness.

I screech loudly for Agnes. 'Agnes! Agnes! Where are you? You Africans can never be trusted to stay in one place! You always dawdle deliberately to annoy me! AGNES!' I reach for a bell on the side table and ring it as hard as my feeble hand can. The silver bell has a melodic tinkling chime to it. Again and again, I ring it, enjoying the melodious sound. Albert bought me the bell in Egypt, long, long ago when we went on a cruise down the Nile, all the way to the Valley of the Kings. 'Agnes! AGNES! AGGG-NES!' My voice becomes a noisy crescendo. Fear grips me that perhaps she has abandoned me. I ring the bell louder.

Drip-drop! Drip-drop! Drip-drop! Drip-Drop! I plonk the bell on the table and plug my ears with my long sinewy fingers to keep out the sound. The overhanging clouds have enveloped the veranda and garden with its greyness. I say a quiet prayer that the sun comes out specifically to drive away the greyness.

Unexpectedly, a smile touches my lips as I recollect that Agnes will later light the hurricane lanterns to give a touch of romance to the veranda as I enjoy a quiet dinner. I predict that the soft glow of the lantern will surely lift me out of my melancholy. But as quickly as the thought pops into my head, I mutter loudly, 'damned circumstances! Damned wheelchair! Damn, damn! 'Agnes! AG-NES! Where are you? Why do you make a habit of disappearing without notifying one that you are about to go on a walk-about like the Australian Aborigines?' My frail voice is shrill and sharp with a sulky childish intonation. It exasperates me that my tone no longer carries any distance or appreciable authority. 'Agnes! Ag-nes! Come here, for heaven's sake!' I strain my eyes towards the far door. I ring the bell loudly.

As I wait impatiently for Agnes to saunter in like a queen, I recollect that my solicitor left for a holiday in England several weeks ago and left money with The League of Mercy for my bills, household essentials, groceries, and staff wages. 'Why haven't those gossipy women come to find out how I am? Damn them!' I say aloud. They only come when they want to persuade me to sell my beach home.

For many years, my friend Isabel and her cohorts of The League of Mercy women have been trying to dictate how I should live my life; unsolicited advice I have adamantly ignored. This is my home, cramped full with all my memories and treasures. Not for all the silver and gold in the world will I ever sell my home. Uninvited, Isabel's voice intrudes and I hear her say, 'Essie dearie, we are all so, so concerned about you. You really must sell this house and go to Nairobi and live in a comfortable, safe home where you will have a nurse at your beck and call! After all, you have no family to inherit your wealth, do you, dearie? Why not sell the blasted lot and enjoy the rest of your life in sheer bliss in Nairobi or in a nice flat in Mombasa? There are plenty of lovely places in Nyali or down in Diani.'

Isabel's pitying voice always irritates me, especially when, in a rather pompous way, she says, 'I am so fortunate to still have all my faculties intact and still able to drive. I know you detest that wheelchair, Essie dear, but we can't change circumstances, can we, dearie! We are the same age, but God knows why I am so healthy while you are confined to that wheelchair!'

Silly woman! Have she forgotten I am confined to the wheelchair because I had a riding accident years ago? And she insists I have no family. Is she bonkers? What about Agnes and her children and grandchildren? What about my driver James and his family? No family? How could I listen to such hogwash from Isabel! What she doesn't know is that I distinctly instructed my lawyer precisely how to divide my property and worldly possessions between my faithful Agnes, James, and a two elderly fishermen who have never failed to bring me fresh fish in all the years I have lived at the coast.

My solicitor was to clearly state in my Will that Agnes and James would inherit the majority of my property. After all, they had become part of my family and indeed, as far as I am concerned, my only family. The two fishermen, Kazungu and Ali, are each to inherit a tidy little nest egg. The rest of my assets are to be sold to pay all my bills, including, of course, funeral costs. Whatever else remains I am bequeathing to The League of Mercy to help other needy souls.

Several years ago, I had made it absolutely clear to my solicitor that I did not wish to be indebted to anyone. Not once have I told any of my inquisitive, prying friends about my Will and my plans! *Never*! Secrets are safest in one's mind. Even my dearest Isabel, with all her subtle probing ways, has failed to unravel my secrets about my property and assets.

Suddenly, in the clarity of my mind, I wonder why I continue to fret about my circumstances; that I must guard every shilling with all my might. When my mind is crystal-clear, I remember that my solicitor has invested my money wisely and that each year I get good returns on my investments. So why do I fret? Old age and a touch of loneliness I suppose.

As I wait impatiently for Agnes, I tell myself how blessed I am to have a lovely home. It is a treasure chest of wonderful collections of artefacts and a collection of happy memories scattered in crooks and crannies; concealed in the midst of the profusion of trees, shrubs, and flowers; sprinkled in the sea beyond my veranda; memories I have faithfully banked, like fat, fat wads of currency, in every available space. To sell my home would be to sell my very life. I shan't ever do that; not for all the tea grown in the highlands of Kenya!

The sudden booming sound of waves startles me. I strain my eyes towards the sea. The tide is fully in. Slowly, the steely greyness that had enveloped the entire expanse of the Indian Ocean begins to give way to gentle sunlight. The rain has lessened in intensity and is now soothing and calming to my frazzled mind. Happier thoughts replace my meandering, mangled ones. Even the drip-drop sounds have disappeared with the rain. Just as I drift into a nap, I hear the melodic voice of Agnes.

'*Memsab*, wake up! Tea time, dear.' I hear her put down the tray, feel her soft hands on my shoulders and feel her gently push my head slightly forward; pick up the pillow and shake it to its proper shape and slip it back to its rightful place. She eases my head back into a comfortable sitting position, making sure my neck is well supported. Patting me on the shoulder, she says sweetly, 'good girl. Now, sit upright so that you can enjoy your tea. It is right here, dear. Have you been a good girl while I was having my afternoon nap?'

I wonder at the audacity of the woman!

'About time too, Agnes!' I mutter crossly, ignoring her cajoling tone. But I quickly forgive her at the thought of our delicious Kenyan tea, a welcome prerequisite any time of day, whether it is sweltering hot or chilly. Agnes hands me my cup and I take a sip. She has made it just as I like it. Unexpectedly, I feel indulgent towards her. 'Has Kazungu or Ali brought any good fish, Agnes?'

'Yes, dear, we have excellent parrotfish today. Will you have it fried or steamed with mashed potatoes and greens and salad?' There is a soothing rhythmic lilt to Agnes' voice. Her gentle hand pats my shoulder.

I know Agnes prides herself on her command of the English language she has learned under my tutelage, from the tender age of fourteen years. But not Queen's English, I am apt to tell her on occasion when she irritates me. I too no longer speak 'correct' English but rather a mishmash of English, Kikuyu, Kiswahili and Giriama created over a period of almost fifty odd years. Over time, Agnes and I have built up an impressive vocabulary of English and Giriama words. 'We must write our own dictionary, Agnes,' I frequently tell her. And each time, predictably, Agnes nods her head in agreement. 'We should do that, dear, before you and I become too old to remember anything.' Her impudence often makes me want to wring her neck, but my total dependency on her inevitably holds me back. There is no room for aristocratic posturing when I can't do a damn thing for myself! Agnes bathes me, powders me and dresses me like a little baby. What would I do without my faithful Agnes? I shudder at the thought that she might one day up and leave me totally alone. I smile sweetly at her. 'This is lovely tea, Agnes. Thank you, dear. I am glad you haven't forgotten what I taught you.'

'You are most welcome, *Memsab*. I think steamed fish served with creamed spinach, mash and salad with olive oil dressing is healthy for you. That is what I shall prepare. What do you think?' She smiles sweetly at me. She refills my empty cup.

'*French fries* rather than mash, Agnes. I may be old with unreliable teeth, but I do not have to eat mashed potatoes every single day of my life, do I? Make the French fries *paper-thin* as I showed you ages ago and not *ugly thick English chips*! Do you hear me, Agnes?' My voice becomes cantankerous and imperious as I gaze haughtily at Agnes, needing to put a stop to any notion she might entertain that she is the Queen of the Roost or even the Queen of England!

'Oh, we are feeling all hoity-toity this afternoon, are we?' says Agnes with a jolly laugh. 'Are you Queen Victoria or Queen Elizabeth today, dearie? Should I curtsy as you taught me ages ago?' A wicked grin spreads across her wrinkle-free face.

The foolish woman has turned the tables on me! Not to be outdone, I glare unflinchingly into her calm, velvety black eyes and say, 'so what if I choose to be Queen Victoria or Queen Elizabeth? *Is it of any consequence to you*? Hurry up and pour me another cup. I am as parched as the Gobi Desert.' I know Agnes is itching to twist my wrinkled neck into a tight coil, tear it of my body and fling it into the sea; I can read the thought in her not-so-innocent eyes.

She pours my tea slowly; deliberately taking her sweet time. When finally done, she says jovially, 'drink your tea, dear, so that I can give you a warm bath. The heat has made you quite sweaty and smelly. I shall use plenty of lily-of-the-valley bath salts and powder to make you smell nice. Your hair needs washing too.'

Agnes peeves me when she talks to me as if I am a mere child. The thirty odd years between us hardly seems to matter to her. The audacity of the woman! The words become a melodious refrain my mind – *the audacity of the woman*! *The audacity of the woman*! I stare into Agnes' smiling eyes and see compassion flood her face. Remorse stabs me. Agnes has worked for me since she was a fourteen-year-old girl and has been a faithful employee to me - no, not an employee but rather a daughter – a mother even. I touch the single strand of precious iridescent black pearls she fastened around my neck this morning. Each time, after she bathes me, she dresses me in my best garments, brushes my wispy hair, and never fails to adorn me with a piece of jewellery to match my outfit. In Agnes's *considered opinion,* I must always be well groomed and well dressed *just in case* I should get unexpected visitors.

Again, remorse stabs at my heart as I recall my habitual annoyance with her over silly, insignificant things. Yet, with all my idiosyncrasies, my barking voice full of demands and complaints, and my rambling fantasies of belonging to an aristocratic lineage hardly ever bothered her until last year when she became so livid with me, I trembled at her rage. For the first time, I saw how much I had angered her. At that time, I gazed back fearfully as I had never seen her so angry before.

Holding her head high like Queen Nefertiti, Agnes said, '*Memsab*, I am not your slave, so you had better treat me with dignity or else I shall quit my job. I have borne your rudeness for a long time, but I shall not do so again. All along, I have been patient with you, but enough is enough. I am a grandmother and as such, you must show me respect.' She continued in an angry voice, 'and if you are truly the Queen's cousin, why are you suffering here in Africa? Why don't you go home to England and live in the Palace with the Queen?'

I was so flabbergasted, I remained silent, wondering how Agnes had the courage to stand before me and speak such words. I hung my head in shame, terribly afraid she would leave me. I muttered an apology, too afraid to look her in the eye. What would I do if she did leave me? Who would take care of me?

But she said in a gentle voice, 'listen, *Memsab*, I know you act very foolishly at times and your words are often unkind, but I know it is because you are worried that you have no family to look after you. But it is wrong for you to treat me harshly and without dignity just because of your worries. By now, you should know that you are like my second mother. And my children consider you their third grandmother. I am sure you know how much we all care for you, but we all expect respect from you. You are not alone in the world. Forgive me for talking to you in this manner, but I have held my peace for too long. It costs you nothing to treat us with dignity.' Agnes stared at me with kind eyes.

I was never more mortified in my life than at that precise moment. Realizing how much I had taken Agnes and my staff for granted, and out of fear of being left all alone, I apologized profusely, tears of shame rolling down my cheeks. Wordlessly, Agnes wrapped her arm around my shoulders.

Now, as my past misdemeanours flood my mind, I thank God that Agnes and James, the driver-cum-gardener-cum-handyman, did not abandon me when my liquid money dried up soon after Albert's death. The rest of the servants - the cook, the laundry girl, and the two gardeners - all left when my solicitor explained that until probate was granted, he could not promise to pay them their wages on time. Agnes and James willingly took on the extra duties and had the solicitor's permission to hire a casual whenever the work became too much for them. After my affairs were sorted out, things settled down nicely. When my solicitor is not gallivanting here and there, he comes regularly with the staff wages, my mail, titillating rumours and news. I have no idea how I would manage without him.

Most of my friends have died, moved into Harrison House, or left the country long ago. On rare occasions, one or two surviving ones at the coast occasionally stop by to have tea, lunch, or dinner. Sometimes, during the holiday months, upcountry friends, their children and grandchildren came to take advantage of my beach house. Even though I no longer enjoy the noise of youngsters, I bear it for the time they are around, heaving a huge sigh of relief when they depart. Agnes is always glad to see the last of them because they keep her busy day and night.

'Agnes dearie, please pour me another cup.' I peer into the greyness. The booming sound of the thundering waves crashing against the coral outcrops is now muted and melodious. As I wait for Agnes to pour my tea, the two wicked words pop up again. *Ominous. Menacing.* Slowly, slowly, I swivel my neck and glance behind me, expecting to see ghosts lurking there in the shadows. Involuntarily, I shiver and stare towards the ocean. Miracles of miracles! I let out a loud 'gracious me! Well, I never! Gracious me, I cannot believe it! Look, Agnes, look at that glorious wonder!'

'What is it, dear?' Agnes stops pouring the tea to follow my pointing finger.

There, astonishingly, above the ocean, is a perfectly arched rainbow, all seven colours visible, sparkling and diffusing across the grey sea. The colours touch the white crest of an incoming wave and turn it into a scintillating wonder of colours. My heart races with joy. The menacing words that have plagued my mind for hours magically disappear. I feel young, joyful.

'Oh, Agnes, look at that splendid rainbow! Isn't it simply gorgeous?' I exclaim, clutching my throat in a conscious, theatrical gesture. I clutch my precious black pearls. They are warm to the touch.

'It is surely beautiful and a good sign because it means you and I will live to be extremely old women, dear.' Agnes laughs happily. She places my bone china teacup on a table ornately inlaid with ivory and ebony, and which we brought from India with the rest of the priceless antiques in the house. Agnes interrupts my thoughts with a slight pat on my back as she say, 'drink your tea before it gets cold.' She pushes me forward to reposition my pillow.

I sit straight as a rod, feeling indulgent towards Agnes. Her infectious buoyant laughter makes me feel elated and contented. 'Agnes, run to the kitchen and bring another cup.' Without questioning why, she disappears, soon returning with a cup. 'Now, bring that wicker chair, put it right next to me, and sit down. You are going to have a cup of tea with me. Old age or not, we must enjoy life, must we not?' A warm feeling of benevolence, of affection, floods my entire being as I reach out my hand and pat Agnes's soft one. 'Agnes, my dear, from now on, you must not call me *Memsab*. It is far too colonial, don't you think? And for your information, the proper Indian way of pronouncing it is *Memsahib*, but the Kenyan colonialists to be quite contrary having always preferred *Memsab*. And from henceforth, you shall call me Esmeralda. Es-me-ral-da. For your information, my name means an emerald, the sacred stone of Venus, the goddess of love. No doubt that is all Greek to you, but never mind, I shall explain it to you another day. If you prefer, you may call me Essie. No more *Memsab*. I'm not living in the golden age of the British Raj, am I? Oh, my dear Agnes, I feel quite liberated! I am sure I could fly if I tried!' I sip my tea, happiness saturating my entire being. I watch Agnes rub her eyes, frowning questioningly at me; disbelief in her eyes, her mouth as wide open as the Indian Ocean.

I chuckle. 'Agnes, stop looking at me as if you are looking at a ghost. Pull up the wicker chair and sit down right next to me! Come on, girl, sit down!' But appearing rooted to the tiled floor, she gazes back, amazement in her eyes. *Ha-Ha*! I chortle inwardly, *I can read your thoughts, Agnes, and you are saying to yourself 'what has come over this quarrelsome, rude old woman? Why is she smiling sweetly and speaking with a jesting, laughter-filled voice like that of an angel?' What revenge is she planning? Yes, Agnes, I can read those thoughts racing across your mind.'* A glow of happiness suffuses my face; a smile creeps up the corners of my lips as I grin into Agnes's astonished eyes. My grin grows wider at the disbelief on Agnes' face.

A ray of hope, like the rainbow playing on the Indian Ocean, sparkles deep within me; I am enlivened, energetic, on top of the world. A thought crosses my mind that some extraordinary human superglue has bonded Agnes and me over the many years; ours is a relationship hard to define, difficult to find adequate words to describe it. It is one of employer-employee, friend-friend, mother-daughter, daughter-mother, an intermingling of many segments of humanity. To be perfectly honest, Agnes is more a mother than a daughter to me. For the past few years, she has played a mother role superbly. I am often petulant as a spoilt child; at times, a crotchety, rude old woman; and occasionally, an angel who sings happily. Through all my foolishness and idiosyncrasies,

Agnes has taken everything in her stride.

'Agnes, don't stand there with your mouth wide enough to let in a whole host of flies. Before you pour your tea and top up mine, nip into my bedroom and bring my tin of Scottish shortbread. We shall celebrate our birthdays today. Never mind if you don't have one, I know I have, but for the life of me, I simply can't remember the date or my age.'

'You celebrated your eighty-fifth birthday last month. ' says Agnes cheerfully.

'Eighty-fifth? Nonsense, my girl. I am a mere thirty-something. I know that for a fact!' Inside my mind, the words chase each other, half-mocking me. Again, I feel I could simply flap my wings and fly. *'Ominous? Menacing? Reduced circumstances?'* I burst into hearty laughter and say aloud, 'what silly, foolish words! What nonsensical words! What niggling little worms!' My eyes rest on the tea tray and I dribble at the thought of the shortbread. The ocean breeze whips up the aroma of my tea and wafts it to my eager nostrils. 'Agnes, don't dawdle! Go bring the shortbread!' I command imperiously. I lift my feeble hand to my mouth, looking guiltily at Agnes. "Agnes, my dear, would you be so kind as to bring the shortbread?'

'I'm going, Esmeralda!' says Agnes, disappearing into the house. Hearing my name pronounced for the first time by Agnes is a shock, an intrusive familiarity, but after a while, the shock becomes a pleasant astonishment. Agnes is soon back, holding out a gaily-coloured tin with a pattern of a Scottish Highland tartan. She removes the cover, revealing perfect triangles of shortbread. 'Here's your shortbread, *Memsab* - I mean Essie.'

Essie? The woman has some nerve! Then I remember that I gave her permission to call me that. I watch her put the tin down, wanting to chivvy her to pour the tea, but I hold my impatient tongue.

'I like the sound of Essie better than Esmeralda. You have a nice name, Essie.' She says, rolling the name round her tongue. On her lips, 'Essie' has a pleasant ring to it, but I actually prefer Esmeralda.

'Thank you, Agnes dear. Now, please pour my tea. I am as parched as the Kalahari Desert.' I give her a smile, stretch out my hand towards hers, needing human warmth and reassurance. She squeezes my hand gently. I let out an audible sigh of contentment, the social and economic distances between us bridged by compassion. Agnes drags the wicker chair nearer to mine. She pours our tea. I sip mine slowly, savouring its subtle taste; our own tea grown in the highlands of Kenya. I am keenly proud that we do not have to import our tea, even though I do enjoy Earl Grey and my solicitor always brings me some from England or the shopping malls in Mombasa.

I look past the garden to the Indian Ocean. The resplendent rainbow is still arched across the horizon, its iridescent colours shimmering across the water, touching the crest of waves and transforming them into phantoms. The phantoms beckon me, but I turn away, face Agnes and say quietly, 'Agnes dear, I want to thank you for the many years you have cared for me, for your patience with me. Above all, I want to thank you for being like a daughter and mother and friend to me.' I see tears sparkle in her eyes. Her hand trembles as she picks up her cup of tea. I hold out the tin of shortbread. She takes one. I take one and nibble it, enjoying its crunchiness. I sip my tea flavoured by my salty tears dripping into it. *Reduced circumstances?* No family? Utter nonsense! I am richer than the Queen of England!

www.ingramcontent.com/pod-product-compliance
Lightning Source LLC
Chambersburg PA
CBHW030130260626
47156CB00008B/2884